burning city

burning city

ariel & joaquin dorfman

random house ⌂ new york

Poetry selections on pages 65, 89, 251, and 252 are from *Poems of Nazim Hikmet*.
Translation copyright © 1994, 2002 by Randy Blasing and Mutlu Konuk.
Reprinted by permission of Persea Books, Inc. (New York).

Published in the United States by Random House Children's Books, a division
of Random House, Inc., New York. Originally published in Great Britain as *The
Burning City* by Random House Children's Books, London, in 2003.

www.randomhouse.com/teens

Library of Congress Cataloging-in-Publication Data
Dorfman, Ariel.
[Burning city]
Burning city / Ariel and Joaquin Dorfman. — 1st U.S. ed.
    p. cm. Originally published in Great Britain in 2003 under title: The burning city.
SUMMARY: Sixteen-year-old Heller Highland, who is living with his grandparents
while his parents are away, burns rubber across Manhattan delivering bad news
by bicycle, and as a summer heat wave melts the city, he is struck by first love.
ISBN 0-375-83203-3 (trade) — ISBN 0-375-93203-8 (lib. bdg.) —
ISBN 0-375-83204-1 (pbk.)
[1. Messengers—Fiction. 2. Bicycles and bicycling—Fiction. 3. Heat waves
(Meteorology)—Fiction. 4. Love—Fiction. 5. Grandparents—Fiction. 6. New York
(N.Y.)—Fiction.] I. Dorfman, Joaquin. II. Title.
PZ7.D6935Bu 2005 [Fic]—dc22
2004009282

Printed in the United States of America 10 9 8 7 6 5 4 3 2 1

RANDOM HOUSE and colophon are registered trademarks of Random House, Inc.

This book is for Isabella

prologue

Heller and his bike burst onto Sixth Avenue, and none of the cars saw him coming.

The screams from the people within those air-conditioned interiors harmonized with the wail of brake pads, tires screeching. To them, Heller was all blur, a silver streak hardly discernible as a teenager on wheels. But to Heller, every car was in clear focus: speed, position, angle. In the second it took him to run the gauntlet across Sixth, not a single driver took him down, not a single bumper made contact with another. It was pure choreography, instant ballet, and before even one motorist or pedestrian had the chance to admire it all, Heller was already eastbound on Twelfth Street.

He didn't stop there. In the blink of a passerby's eye he'd crossed Fifth, once again unscathed, making tracks for University Place.

1:35 in the afternoon and he was already ahead of schedule. 1:36, just about to cross University Place, when Heller saw Bruno on the corner, standing less than twenty yards away, unmistakable despite the uniform. Bruno the Bruiser.

Their eyes locked.

Heller needed only a moment to see the badge, the nightstick, the gun hanging from Bruno's belt. Needed one more moment to wonder if the safety was off. Needed one last moment to change direction.

Detour.

Heller popped his wheels off the curb, altered his course, pedaled with traffic up to Union Square. Past the bars and garbage bags on the sidewalk waiting for collection. Past the lunchtime patrons of Burger King. Past the Knights of Jerusalem on Fourteenth Street, preaching to the world about the white devil and a return to the truth. Past the skateboarders and bums lying about in the summer sun, past all that . . .

People yelled and jumped out of his way, squirrels joining them in the mad dash for safety. Heller let speed fuel his bike, legs beating against the pedals. He might have noticed a man sitting at a makeshift table, books strewn about its surface. He might have noticed this man's look, calm in the midst of the frenzy of movement in Heller's wake. He might have noticed the curious expression dancing in this man's dark brown eyes, set in the features of a face filled with experience, a very slight dent in his left cheek, as though the bone had started to cave in. He might have noticed the man's unassuming stance as he blazed past. Might have noticed . . .

But he didn't.

Although this man, without question, noticed Heller.

Boom. The man watched as Heller tore himself out of the park, through a double-edged stream of uptown/downtown traffic, cut across a corner, narrowly skirting a cluster of tourists who felt lucky to have avoided an accident. Heller knew there was no accident and there was no luck. All the tourists saw was his back to them, a boy on his bike, black T-shirt with the words SOFT TIDINGS printed in friendly, light blue letters.

The detour now behind him, Heller turned south, down toward St. Mark's Place, made a left.

The sun was at a slant, and its light created shadows out of everything. Heller biked through it all, his silhouette casting itself on the tattoo parlors, used-CD stores, past the late Coney Island High club, past the homeless and Hampton punks pretending to bum around for the weekend, past Yaffa Café . . . into Alphabet City, where the neighborhood turned sketchy and prices dropped along with expectations.

Heller had arrived.

His right arm tightened, hit the brakes.

Dead stop.

Right there on Avenue B.

He jumped off his bike, hit the button on his digital watch.

Checked the time.

"Thirteen fifty-two," Heller whispered. "Damn Bruno."

He was going to have to do better in the future.

The streets had somehow become empty. A few cars, a random bodega owner standing outside his store, waiting for business to pick up. Other than that, stillness. It was as though the birds had left to find some other city to call home.

Heller chained his bike to a NO PARKING sign. He reached into his pocket and pulled out an ambiguously light green card. . . .

4 x 8.

Heller read over the details.

His expression melted. He walked toward the apartment building in front of him, suddenly alert to something other than movement or speed. Resolute and controlled because reality had suddenly seeped back into the world.

The card had left out the apartment number. It happened on occasion, due to the fault of the client or some sort of clerical error. Heller searched the buzzers on the outside door, looking for a specific name, specific destiny.

Half the buzzers were unmarked.

Heller searched for a brief while longer, the silence of an otherwise noisy city growing all around him.

The door to the building opened without warning. A middle-aged man stood in place of the door, mustached, with a rehearsed look on his face. Superintendent, to be sure.

"Can I help you, son?"

It seemed like a rhetorical question.

"I'm looking for Mr. Benjamin Ibo, please."

The superintendent regarded Heller closely, sensed that something was wrong. "He expecting you?"

"No."

The super nodded sadly. "Three flights up, turn left, apartment thirty-five."

"Thank you."

Heller made his way up the stairs, preparing for his first encounter of the day. With each floor, he felt as though a layer of himself were peeling away and shedding onto the dusty steps.

APT. NO. 35.

Heller knocked on the door three times.

He waited.

From behind the door at the end of the hall a dog barked, scratched its nails against the wood. The door opened, and a fifty-year-old man with oily gray hair and wide eyes stuck his head out, holding a large greyhound by his side.

"What do you want?" he snapped. "What are you doing here in my HOUSE?"

"I'm here to see Mr. Benjamin Ibo," Heller said calmly.

"I thought so!" declared the man triumphantly before slamming his door closed.

Peace was restored to the hallway. Heller was sweating, a staleness in the air sticking to him. Finally, Benjamin Ibo answered the knock.

Heller knew from the card that Benjamin Ibo was Nigerian. Twenty-some years old. Heller didn't need any sort of statistic to know that Benjamin was a man well traveled. He could see it in his eyes, saw it in most of the people he visited.

Benjamin Ibo stood before him, leaning against the threshold with one hand on the doorknob. Majestic face and dark brown eyes matching his skin, green soccer jersey hanging over his body.

Gray boxer shorts.

Neither of them spoke. Finally:

"What's up, then?" Benjamin asked.

Heller took a breath. "Soft Tidings . . ."

Benjamin already knew, must have felt it when he woke up that day. He nodded, let Heller into the apartment, and closed the door. . . .

The lock engaged itself.

chapter one

Heller thought the entire world was going to melt that summer.

It was the Fourth of July and all of Manhattan was sweating. It was coming out of the streets, buildings, faucets; even the Hudson River could be heard for miles, begging for a drink, something to keep it cool. Radios reported the weather out of habit. Sleeping couples woke up to damp sheets. Construction workers went without their shirts and stockbrokers loosened their ties with quiet envy. Tourists complained, ice-cream vendors smiled, and mercury climbed steadily up tired thermometers.

Heller Highland saw all of this, and that which he couldn't see he simply knew. School had been out for just over a month. He sat on the roof of his building and kept his eyes on the sky, due southeast. Glass of water in his left hand, ice already dissolved, even in the cool of the evening. Airplane lights traveled past, left and right, fireflies of the twentieth century—

Twenty-first century, Heller corrected himself silently. *It's two thousand and one; twenty-first century. . . .*

He took a sip of water. Waited for the fireworks to start. Independence Day.

There was no American flag in his right hand. Just a telegram. No red, white, or blue. Just an elegantly embossed message on an ambiguously light green card; 4 x 8. Heller was barely aware he was holding it. Just watched the sky. An unchanging Manhattan skyline. The sounds of the city kept him company. The distant blast of traffic, pedestrians, and the hum of a thousand air conditioners and fans, all in the same key.

A breeze managed to find its way into the city, and Heller's blond hair lifted itself, thankful. Heller smiled. He stopped. Smiled again, stopped, smiled, bit his lip and stopped. A few seconds later the wind died down, and Heller was left in his chair, on his roof, in his city of millions.

"Fireworks are late," came a voice behind him.

Heller didn't turn around. "Any minute now, I'm sure."

His grandfather, Eric, walked up next to him, stood for a while, glanced down.

"Telegram?"

"Yes."

"Soft Tidings?"

"Yeah."

"I thought you had the day off."

"It's from Mom and Dad."

"Really? What's it say?"

"Haven't read it."

Eric kept quiet, thought about it. Then:

"They should be coming back soon."

"I'd like to think so. . . ."

Grandfather forced a chuckle. "You make it sound like they're dead."

"I do not," Heller said. "I just know how it can be with them."

The two of them watched the sky. An ambulance cried in the distance. Heller wondered at the emergency. Thought about a phone call at three in the morning. Thought about a family waiting for news thousands of miles away. Thought too much.

"Did you see Silvia today?" Eric asked.

". . . I stopped by the coffee shop," Heller said cautiously. "She was there."

"When do I get to meet her?"

"Soon."

"I know your grandmother's been wanting to meet her for a long time. . . . Heller?"

"I know how she feels. . . ."

"Heller?" Eric repeated, voice softer this time.

"Yeah?"

"We should have had some sort of celebration, you know."

"I like celebrating like this."

"Are you happy living with your grandmother and me?"

"You know I am."

"Are you sure?"

"You know I am," Heller said.

"Mom and Dad are fine, I promise."

"Now *you* make it sound like they're dead."

"I don't think you're hearing me right."

An explosion tore the night apart and a hot blast of red lit the air. Heller jumped inadvertently. Within three seconds the entire night was filled with a thousand lights, imitation stars, fireworks mirroring the glow of apartments and office buildings.

"Hey, there they are," Eric said.

"Boom, boom."

"Happy Fourth of July, Heller."

Heller nodded.

"I'll go get your grandmother."

Heller listened to his grandfather's footsteps head for the stairs. The sky erupted over and over, and Heller felt the smile return, bit his lip. "Eric?"

The footsteps halted. Twelve deafening fireworks were released at once.

"Mom and Dad say they're doing fine."

"What?"

Heller cleared his throat. "Happy Fourth of July."

He couldn't see his grandfather but could sense him nodding as he said, "Happy birthday, Heller. . . . Sweet sixteen . . ."

The ribbons of light cascaded over the city. Blast after blast, the sky rained down on Heller and the rest of the country. The world seemed to be getting smaller, the summers hotter, and despite the air-conditioning, the city continued to sweat.

Heller brought the glass of water to his lips and realized it was empty.

The entire world was going to melt that summer.

There was no doubt about this in Heller's mind.

chapter two

Heller made it down Lafayette Street and onto Kenmare in one piece. He chained his bike to the usual NO PARKING sign. It was approaching 9:00 a.m., and he was already sweating; the sun wasn't planning on saying uncle. Heller took a long tug at his water bottle, then gave his bike seat an affectionate pat.

The streets were thick with people, workers and tourists, weaving in and out between construction detours and hot-dog stands. Heller walked eastward, passed a group of students from his high school moving toward him. Three girls, one guy. They walked by, not recognizing him, and Heller overheard one of them say—

". . . You get more channels with a satellite package. . . ."

—before their smiles were swept into the crowd. Heller stopped, glanced back for a moment, then walked through the metal door to 1251.

It was almost time to get to work.

What Heller Highland knew about the rest of the employees at Soft Tidings didn't amount to much. They were all out of high school. Some were in college, others weren't; a diploma was almost a must for employment. A few of them were from New York, most were first-generation Americans; knowing a second language was another near-necessity at Soft Tidings. A select amount worked part time, the rest worked full time; all of them were required to wear Rollerblades.

Heller didn't meet any of the above conditions.

Everyone else did, and they made it their business to make sure Heller didn't forget it:

"Well, if it isn't the bicycle thief!"

Heller stepped into the main offices of Soft Tidings and instantly recognized the voice of Rich Phillips. Didn't need to turn and see the wide grin, malicious eyes half covered by soft brown hair. Rich Phillips was senior staff, twenty-two, the oldest of the messengers. He set the example for the rest, and Rich Phillips never missed a chance to make an example of Heller.

Heller tried to get through the room as quickly as possible, but Rich was already in front of him, Rollerblades slung over his shoulder. He stood at six two, a full half foot taller than Heller. The rest of the staff gathered around to watch.

"Happy birthday, Heller," Rich said. "You get a new pacifier?"

A room full of laughter.

". . . No."

"Didn't spend it with your girl, Heller?" came a voice from out of the crowd.

"I think Heller's a bit old for make-believe," Rich announced, receiving a hero's applause from the other workers. Then, to Heller: "No pacifier, no girl, what *did* you do to celebrate your Fourth of July?"

Heller kept his eyes to the ground.

"Oh, that's right, you got a telegram, didn't you? How are your parents?"

"Fine."

"Mom and Dad enjoying themselves in Africa?"

"I guess."

"Well, guess what?"

Heller didn't answer.

Rich straightened himself into the perfect pose of authority. "Dimitri wants to see you in his office, right now."

"Richard?"

Everyone turned to find Iggy Platonov sitting at his desk, legs kicked up, leafing through multicolored slips of paper. His unassuming demeanor hung off him like a tailored jacket. Even though he was only a few years older than Heller, he somehow looked to be approaching thirty, and it was easy for the rest of them to forget that there was no decade of difference between them and Iggy.

"Iggy." Rich's composure was taken down a notch. "I didn't see you there."

Iggy shrugged. "I have a gift for these things. It's called the gift of the general manager. And along with this gift, it is the general manager's job to relay any orders from Dimitri. Not you, Rich."

Rich nodded, unperturbed.

"And as for the rest of you, you can get off Heller's back about this girlfriend thing. He does have a woman all his own. Her name is Silvia. She works at Buns 'n' Things, and she's a knockout. So don't think that just because Heller doesn't run his mouth around you perverts that he's got no place else to do it."

A strange wave of brotherly pride found its way into Rich's face. "All right, Casanova." He held up his hands, backing down from Heller. "You should bring her by sometime. Sounds like someone I'd like to meet . . . you know what I'm saying?"

Heller cleared his throat. He looked around for help. Nobody offered any.

A loud beep from Iggy's computer punctuated the silence.

"All right, Richard." Iggy sat up, face turning to its business side. "We've got a baby in Dubai and twins in Belarus. Our new Internet spots have doubled our foreign market and the population seems to be doubling by the minute, so you're on newborn service today. Fill out your morning time sheet and get ready to work."

Richard scowled, looked as though he might object.

"Garland!" Iggy called out to an unseen messenger in the crowd. "I've got a typhoon in Taiwan. Heller's going to be a bit late getting out there today, so I need you to take this one."

"Bad news ain't my job!" came the protest from the back of the room. "Heller's our angel of death, not me!"

"It's one message, Garland. We'll have you back on weddings and promotions once we get back . . . all right?"

No further arguments were heard.

"All right, everyone!" Iggy clapped his hands three times. "Let's go, let's go!"

All at once, the office transformed into Grand Central Station. A mix of voices and movements dead set on schedules and appointments with no apparent order to the activity. Phones, faxes, printouts, receipts passed from hand to hand. It would be like this for most of the morning.

A paper airplane sailed past Heller's face. He turned to see Iggy watching him with playfully accusing eyes.

"Heller . . . I don't see any Rollerblades." Iggy's eyes turned serious, voice stern. "My father wants to see you in his office, right now."

Heller nodded. He shuffled toward the door at the far end, past the rows of desks, phones, and computers. He felt everyone's eyes, sensed their smiles despite their focus on that day's orders. He bit his lip. Reached for the doorknob, opened, stepped through, and closed the door behind him.

chapter three

The name was embossed on a plaque that sat at the front of his desk. Heller wondered what the point was; Dimitri Platonov was the boss. Creator and head of Soft Tidings. The employees knew it. Anyone from the outside would have known it, otherwise they wouldn't be in his office. Dimitri Platonov was clearly the name of Heller's boss, clearly in charge of Soft Tidings, and he was clearly not pleased to see Heller that morning.

"Heller." His Russian accent was slight and his tone stern. "Mr. Highland. Have a seat. Please."

Heller did as he was told, sat down. He waited.

Dimitri was heavyset, features of a bulldog. Personality to match, most would say. Eyebrows as thick as his mustache, face set in stone. He was a businessman. Wore his suit as though he had been born with it. Someone told Heller that he had once seen Dimitri crying. Quiet tears, late one night when nobody else was around.

Heller cleared his throat. Dimitri cleared his, leaned forward.

"Happy birthday, Heller."

Heller nodded.

"Your parents wanted me to take extra pains to see that your birthday telegram was delivered. . . . Good to hear from them?"

"Yeah."

"They're good people, your parents."

Heller nodded slightly.

"Do you know what I did yesterday?"

Heller shook his head. The office was quiet, shelves filled with various collectors' items from the Home Shopping Network. Dolls, decorative cups, and Elvis plates watched him silently.

"I got digital cable installed on my television. . . ."

Dimitri picked up a remote control and pointed it at the flat-screen TV across the room. It clicked, lit up. Rambo spraying bullets into a Vietnamese camp . . .

"With the package they gave me, I get HBO, HBO2, Showtime. Cinemax one, two, and three. The Movie Channel, Starz! . . ."

He flipped through the channels as he spoke: Cover Girl commercials, bombs in Israel, Jerry Springer . . .

"I get the Sci Fi Channel. Comedy Central. MTV, MTV2, VH1, E!, ESPN, ESPN2, ESPN Classic. Oxygen, the women's network; WE, the other women's network; Lifetime, which I suspect is a women's network; and news channels. I've got CNN, MSG, MSNBC, Fox News, not to speak of the network television reports and the local news. Round-the-clock coverage of what's going on in every country. I can keep on top of events, Heller, what's going on in the world. . . ."

He flipped past an insurance commercial, car commercial,

antidepressant commercial. Bob Saget telling one of the Olsen twins not to be afraid of her dentist appointment, that everything was going to be all right . . .

"If I miss a news report in the morning, I can catch it on a broadcast set to Western/Pacific time three hours later. And if I need to leave the office in the middle of a breaking story, I can actually *freeze the image*. . . ."

Dimitri hit a button on the remote control, and the screen did, in fact, freeze in the middle of an MTV video featuring four or five R & B singers decked out in jewelry and designer clothes, sitting on the stoop of a housing project. Dimitri stared at the screen, not saying anything. Heller shifted in his seat and made as if to speak. Dimitri held up his hand, indicating for him to wait.

Heller waited.

Finally, Dimitri resumed play on the TV screen, continued, "And I can get right back to the story without having missed any of it. Very impressive, don't you think?"

"You get more channels with satellite," Heller said quietly.

Dimitri frowned, turned off the television, and leaned back, arms folded. "I got another call from the police department, Heller. I said to them that I did not want to know, but they went right ahead and told me. So, please, now you tell me: what made you think it was a wise idea to take a shortcut through the Warner Brothers' building during midtown's peak hours?"

Heller sat, mute and unmoving.

"Several people were almost hurt diving out of your way. A very important executive heading to an even more important meeting spilled an entire cup of coffee on himself. Lucky for you nobody was injured, and the coffee was not hot enough to seriously burn the man. Still . . . what the hell were you thinking, Heller?"

"I had to make time . . ." Heller's voice was barely audible over the hum of the air-conditioning. "We never deliver messages to midtown, but the uptown offices were short staffed, so I had to make time. I cut two point three minutes off the normal time it would have taken me to make the delivery."

"Heller, you don't drive an ambulance. The world doesn't rest on your handlebars. Cyclists are a danger to pedestrians—that is why I require my employees to wear Rollerblades. Now, no more screwing around, Heller; when are you going to ditch that bicycle and get yourself a pair of Rollerblades?"

"I bought a pair of Rollerblades—"

"Two months ago, Heller. I expect you to also *wear* them."

"They were stolen."

"Buy some new ones."

"I can't afford them."

"Rollerblades?"

"If I buy Rollerblades, I have to buy wrist guards and knee pads and a helmet—"

"Don't I pay you?"

"I'm saving my money."

"And you don't ever buy yourself lunch, a cup of coffee, new brake pads for your bicycle?"

"I need those. . . ."

"You need Rollerblades. I could easily buy you a pair and take it out of your paycheck, but I just can't do that.

You know how your father feels about fairness, and you know what I owe your father."

"My father's a long way from here."

"So was Leningrad. . . . When I first came to this country, I didn't have anybody; no friends, no family, no sweet young girl would have even thought to serve me coffee, I can tell you that much. Now I have my own place of business in Manhattan, with branches in Queens, Brooklyn, and Long Island, along with a Web site that gets thousands of hits a day. I have an apartment on the Upper West Side overlooking Central Park. I have a BMW, a physical therapist—and digital cable with over one hundred and fifty channels. You were born in America, Heller, and you don't appreciate the fact that you can buy Rollerblades. . . ."

Heller opened his mouth, closed it. He glanced at the clock on the wall.

9:17.

Dimitri's phone rang; once, twice, three times before he lifted the receiver.

"Soft Tidings, news with a personal touch; this is Dimitri Platonov. . . ." A moment of listening. Dimitri shot Heller a glance, attended for another few seconds, then quietly pressed the speaker button on the phone. The voice of an old Puerto Rican woman filled the room:

". . . when he delivered the news, he was just so kind and considerate and helpful. I don't know how I would have taken the death of my nephew if he hadn't been so understanding. I just wanted to make sure that you knew what a good kid he is, and if he hasn't been promoted already, then he should be. . . ."

Dimitri kept his eyes on Heller. "Do you have his name?"

"I wrote it down, but I can't find the paper. It's such a mess around here."

"Was it Heller?"

"Oh, yes!" The voice on the other end was filled with warm affection. "Heller, that's the one."

"Yes, that's the one."

Heller smiled, bit his lip, stopped.

"I'll make sure he gets your message," Dimitri continued.

"He's such a considerate young man, such a good listener. I felt I could have just talked and talked and talked—"

"I'll see he gets the message. You make sure to ask for him if you ever need us again. Goodbye."

Dimitri hung up, stared across the desk, sighing. He picked up the remote control and contemplated it. Then: "You do what you do very well, Heller. The only reason you got this job in the first place was because I felt indebted to your parents. I didn't think you'd last one week here, to tell you the truth. As it turns out, you handle tragedy very well. I don't know why, but for every complaint from the police department, I've received twenty phone calls from satisfied customers. . . . You are definitely your father's son."

Heller glanced down at his sneakers.

"But you are still working for me, and I have to take into account that sooner or later your reputation on the streets is going to come into conflict with your reputation as an employee of Soft Tidings. I don't want that to happen any more than you, so I am putting the foot down. . . ."

Heller lifted his head.

"If I get any reports that you and your bike have caused anybody any bodily injury, you're fired. You have until next Thursday to get yourself a pair of Rollerblades. I want Rollerblades. I want knee pads. I want wrist guards. I want you off that bicycle, Heller. It's time you joined the rest of the team . . . all right?"

Heller nodded.

"All right, get to work. Iggy has your first assignment."

Heller stood up, walked to the door. Dimitri's voice stopped him, his hand on the doorknob:

"Heller—"

Turning around, Heller saw that Dimitri had resumed his channel surfing.

"Drink a lot of water, stay hydrated. It's going to be a hot one this week."

"Okay."

"Close the door behind you."

Heller did as he was told.

Back in the office, Heller was met with quiet smirks and taunting eyes through the bustle of office work. He stood still and felt the news of Dimitri's warning spread across the room, filling every corner, washing back into him, and spreading like a lead weight through his body. His eyes went from face to face, wide grins reminding him of a high school cafeteria.

Heller caught Rich staring at him from a distance, his face hard.

He made his way to Iggy's desk.

It was like wading through shit.

"One week, Heller," Iggy said, handing him a few green cards and receipts.

"Rollerblades," Heller answered.

Iggy nodded. Heller walked toward the office door, where Rich was stationed, smoking a cigarette, Rollerblades slung over his shoulder. As Heller walked past him, Rich turned and walked alongside, down the cavernous stairs to the ground level of 1251 Kenmare. They descended in silence and walked out the front door, onto the streets.

The sudden heat, traffic, and movement overwhelmed Heller. Rich stood by him, calm and unmoving, breathing out the last reserve of smoke and crushing his cigarette underfoot.

"Another day of death and sorrow . . . ," he said.

Heller strode north, breath short, heart beating double its normal rate.

"You like your job, don't you, Heller?" Rich called after him.

Heller stopped. Didn't turn back, just kept perfectly still.

"I enjoyed it myself, bike boy," Rich added. "I look forward to taking back my old route once you're gone."

Heller continued onward, jostled left and right, small and insignificant in a world preoccupied with more important things. Dimitri's words buzzed around him. Billboards and storefronts boasted the latest in just about everything a person could want. Cabs and buses were plastered with movie posters, cologne ads, and ads for dot-com companies.

His bike was waiting for him. Heller got on his knees, fumbled with the lock, sweat covering his hands, dripping into his eyes.

He freed his bike, wrapped the chain around his seat. The city pressed down on him.

Jumping on his bicycle, Heller let out a deafening scream and pedaled directly into oncoming traffic.

It was 9:30 and time to get to work.

chapter four

Heller saw the approaching taxi, heard its horn blaring, didn't let it bother him.

"YOU'RE GOING TO SWERVE FIRST!" he screamed.

It was true. The taxi was going to swerve first because the driver thought he had only three seconds until impact and Heller knew he had four.

The taxi swerved, almost running into a parked garbage truck. Heller missed the taxi's bumper by an inch or so, a fantastic, raw glee coursing through him. The pressure in his chest was gone, evaporated along with any misgivings about the city's fate.

Heller turned north on Lafayette, spotted a long stretch of deserted sidewalk on the other side of the street, and cut through the traffic, onto the curb, and directly in front of a Soft Tidings employee.

Garland Green. His blue eyes turned to slits, glinting bright like the network of wire braces fused to his teeth. Garland pressed down on his Rollerblades, increasing his speed to catch up to Heller, now clearly glad to be delivering what should have been Heller's first message of the day.

Heller knew Garland didn't stand a chance. He caught sight of an approaching dog walker: a blonde in spandex pants, the leashes of seven different dogs in one hand. Heller sped past her, barking at the dogs, letting his spit fly through the air. The dogs answered with their own declaration of war, freed themselves from the blonde, and gave chase to Heller and Garland.

Heller stood on the pedals, pumped up the speed. A passing tour bus slowed down, out-of-towners witness to this New York spectacle, snapping pictures with disposable cameras. Heller took one moment to smile and wave before noticing a steady flow of traffic heading west.

Just as the dogs were about to overtake him, Heller turned to move with the flow, grabbed on to the open window of a speeding car, stopped pedaling, using its momentum to make the bricks and fire escapes a massive blur. He glanced over his shoulder to see Garland surrounded by mutts, covered in drool and a chorus of barking.

Heller held fast to his ride, looked through the window. The driver was a young man with slicked-back hair, expensive sunglasses wrapped around his face. He had sharp Italian features. Heller watched him bounce his head to bass-filled music, lyrics screaming guns, drugs, and money.

"COME ON!" Heller yelled at the driver. *"You can do better'n this!"*

The driver turned his head, cool gone in an instant. "What the hell?"

"LET'S SPEED THIS UP, SLICK!"

"WHAT THE HELL YOU DOING, YO?"

Heller let out a loud burst of laughter, echoes of a war cry rattling his body.

"LET GO, MAN!" the driver yelled.

"YOU FIRST!"

"WHAT?"

"COME ON, MAN!" Heller urged as the car picked up speed. "WE MAKE A GREAT TEAM!"

"THIS IS MY FATHER'S FAVORITE CAR. LET GO!"

"RED LIGHT!"

The driver turned his head back to the road and shrieked.

He slammed on the brakes with both feet.

The car screeched to a halt.

Heller didn't.

He and his bike went straight through the intersection, slicing through lower Broadway traffic, arms held wide at his sides, eyes closed. A thousand sounds enveloped him, and an instant later he was safely across, turning right, leaving the momentarily halted traffic behind.

He bounced his front wheel onto the sidewalk. Outside the Tisch Building film students were gathered, discussing the latest Kevin Smith film.

Heller pressed down on the pedals, drove his faithful bike forward.

The students had less than an instant to scream, dive out of the way. Heller cut through the crowd of up-and-coming artists, a fresh grin stuck to his face so hard it brought pain to his cheeks.

Good pain. Rewarding.

Heller made a hard left. His bike tilted at forty-five degrees, defying gravity, then righted itself as he coursed between two cars on Waverly Place, swerved out of the path of a hot-dog stand and down the street.

He wasn't intending to go through the park—the address he was looking for was on Christopher Street, and going through Washington Square would take away a near thirty seconds from Heller's schedule. But then, out of the corner of his eye, he saw them: a close-knit couple, arms locked, lips pressed together, standing in a perfect spotlight of sunshine at the park's entrance.

Content. Pleased. Perfect.

Heller's watch told him he was a full minute ahead of schedule.

He let out another yell, cut left. The couple didn't see him coming, didn't see him speed past, so close Heller could have run his fingers through the girl's hair with one slight motion of his hand. All they felt was a sudden breeze lift their hair slightly, an awareness of something happening. They opened their eyes, smiling.

Heller sped along the bench-lined path leading to the center of the park. Sunlight made its way through the trees, and the wind rocked his face as pigeons scattered. An old man with a wrinkled suit and white scruff adorning his neck looked up from his drink and raised his hand up in the air:

"Yeah, bike boy!" he cheered. "You show 'em what speed really means, you lunatic! GRAND TOUR!"

"TO THE GRAND TOUR!" Heller cried over his shoulder.

The world was coming alive, and Heller kept on. Past the statue of Garibaldi, into the wide open square of the park, where the jugglers, students, bums, preachers, families, drug dealers, and musicians made their home.

"Bike boy!" one of the performers announced.

"Bike boy!" came the chorus of a few of the drummers

seated near the fountain, oversized T-shirts worn like robes. "Where you been?"

"Get off the bike, asshole!"

"Grand Tour, bike boy!"

Laughter and salutations mixed with jeers quickly spread as Heller coasted his way over the shimmering concrete. Looking right, he saw Bruno the Bruiser with his nightstick drawn, poking and prodding a man sitting at a makeshift table, books strewn about its surface, calm expression dancing in his brown eyes.

Heller took a deep, angry breath. He locked eyes with the book vendor and, for an instant, forgot where he was. Thought he recognized something in the man's face, the way he stood out in the crowd, a dent resting softly in his left cheek. Caught in his stare, Heller almost felt like he wasn't speeding on his bike at all, but standing still as the rest of the park moved about him.

"Bike boy!" A shirtless Haitian stood up on the wall surrounding the fountain. Water cascaded from behind him. Small droplets found their way through the air and onto his back. "I heard they put you in jail, man!"

The Haitian's comment brought Heller back to the moment just as quickly as he'd left.

"You been behind bars, bike boy?" the Haitian called out.

Heller let out a defiant laugh and, as if to prove his point, doubled his speed. He shoved the entire world out of his peripheral sight and aimed for Bruno.

Cut off Bruno in midsentence, snatched his police hat from off his head, and kept pedaling. Heard Bruno swear and start to run after him. Applause from all over the park.

A Frisbee was launched, aimed at Heller's head, missing and landing in a garbage can. Heller answered this call by sending Bruno's hat flying into a crowd of students juggling a Hacky Sack.

A world of noise at his back, Heller exploded out of the park, past The Arch and back onto Waverly Place. He left them all behind to love him, hate him, speak of him for days to come. Riding his bike and tearing through the concrete streets and alleyways of the city, this was where Heller felt close to the world. Through red lights and one-way streets, ignoring the sun, the sweat, polar ice caps, slaughter overseas, lost votes, Air Jordans, AIDS, and that slow countdown that everyone felt in the back of their heads, throats, hearts.

The entire world was going to melt that summer, and it was in those moments that Heller was more than willing to melt with it.

Right on schedule.

chapter five

Almost four in the afternoon—Chinatown.

Heller's bike slid to a halt, perfect break speed.

He leaped off, hit the button on his watch. Numbers froze. He looked at the results, staring right back at him.

Twelve minutes, forty-six seconds.

"Damn it," Heller murmured through the flower clamped between his teeth.

Heller chained his bike to a parking meter.

It was his seventh and final delivery of the day.

The door opened an instant after knocking.

It was as though Mrs. Chiang had been expecting him.

"Mrs. Chiang?"

She turned out to be a small, delicately featured woman. A dress decorated with flowers. Dark hair with traces of gray, done up in a bun. Strangely lucid eyes.

It was as though she had been expecting him.

"Is something the matter?"

She was drying her hands with a dishrag.

"I think you know why I'm here," Heller said. He

gently took the dishrag out of her hand and gave her the flower. She stared at it for a moment, lost herself in carnation petals.

She looked back into his eyes and nodded.

"Is anybody else home?" he asked.

"I only have one son," she answered slowly. "That's all."

"Is there a place where we can both sit?"

Mrs. Chiang walked into the apartment. Heller followed, closing the door behind him.

The apartment was sparsely furnished, though Heller suspected that years had been spent living there staring at the same decorations, waiting. A round table in the middle of the living room, scattered chairs. No sofa. No couch. No futon. Along the few shelves and windowsills were inexpensive-looking toys and models. Miniature desks, foul-looking garden gnomes, obscenely cheerful nativity scenes, crucifixes, small porcelain frogs. The afternoon sunlight made the walls look soft, malleable.

Mrs. Chiang motioned to the small table by the window. They sat. She played absently with a small wooden horse. Its painted eyes looked every which way at once. Outside, the city continued to weave in and out of traffic, unravel and sustain itself.

"Are you sure?" she asked finally. "How can you be sure?"

"This was the only information your brother gave us. . . ."

Heller slid the card across the table. Mrs. Chiang picked it up. Read it. A bird landed on the windowsill, watched them. Flew away. Mrs. Chiang put the card down silently. Heller watched her sit, taking in all that he could.

"There's something in that message that your brother doesn't say," Heller told her. "Your son was a good man."

Mrs. Chiang gave a half nod, toyed with that wooden horse for a while. "I hadn't heard from my son in twelve years," she managed. "How old are you?"

"Sixteen."

"I haven't heard from my son since you were four . . . since before you could manage a sentence with your hands." She looked out the window. "They don't let them write. But I knew what he was doing in there. My son and all the other prisoners in the *lao gai*. Do you know what *lao gai* means?"

"Reeducation camps."

Mrs. Chiang's face gave way to surprise.

"My father told me . . . ," Heller said.

"That's right . . . and the only connection I had with him were these. . . ."

She stood up, still holding on to the wooden horse, swept her arms across the length of the apartment. "Do you know how much these cost?" Pointing to an ashtray shaped like a jack-o'-lantern: "One dollar." Pointing to a cradle carved out of wood to resemble a mother's arms: "One dollar." Pointing to a small stuffed animal: "One dollar . . ."

Her arms fell to her sides.

Heller kept his eyes glued to her, never saying a word, never moving a muscle.

"Because my son wasn't paid . . . he was hardly fed. . . . Cheap . . . Life is cheap."

She pointed toward the kitchen this time. Heller looked through that open doorway over to the refrigerator. A drawing of a butterfly was pinned to its surface, scrawled in crayon. One wing red, the other totally white.

"My son made that at the age of seven," she said. "When

33

his father brought in a wounded butterfly, half a wing left to its body . . . I don't think he ever stopped thinking about it. . . ." She lowered her voice then, trying to hide something from the figurines watching from their places on the shelves. "Where do you think I found the butterfly again?"

Heller's eyes never left hers. "It's carved into the bottom of the horse, Mrs. Chiang."

She smiled sadly. Mrs. Chiang smiled sadly and turned the horse over on the table to reveal the same asymmetrical butterfly carved into the belly of that silent, all-knowing toy.

Heller looked up from the evidence: "I don't think he ever stopped speaking to you. . . ."

Mrs. Chiang sank into her chair.

Heller watched her shoulders rise and fall with her every breath. He waited for the tears to come. Her eyes grew moist, but not a drop spilled onto the table. So they both waited there at that table, in the middle of that apartment, not sure what to expect next.

The clock on the wall was the only thing that bothered to move.

A calendar on an opposing wall was the only thing moving faster than that.

chapter six

The door closed behind him, accompanied by the familiar ring of the bell. A few people turned their heads, looked up from books or unpublished screenplays. For the most part, Heller's entrance into Buns 'n' Things went unnoticed. The soft sounds of coffee cups continued, and the quiet blinking of seasonally misplaced Christmas lights accompanied Heller to his seat. He sat down, looked out the window, tapped his fingers nervously against the marble table.

Heller didn't like the place. Didn't enjoy SoHo to begin with. South of Houston. Too much of it seemed to be impeccably clean. Designer stores. Expensive, mechanically superior watches, hundred-dollar jeans, thousand-dollar dresses, inflatable furniture. Sometimes the neighborhood seemed as cold as the stainless-steel construction of the bars and restaurants.

Buns 'n' Things had a certain warmth to it, but the world of Art Deco galleries and commissioned artists always found a way to get in through the wall of windows that covered the storefront. The coffee was certainly far too expensive for far too little; a watery house blend with only one free refill.

And Heller didn't enjoy coffee to begin with. Caffeine was a dehydrating agent, not good for the circulation and completely impractical for his work. Didn't even like the taste much. Just didn't like coffee . . .

"Would you like to see a menu?"

Heller turned away from the window. That Latin accent was accompanied by soft, dark eyes and black hair. Cut just past shoulder length, straight and shiny. She wore a red shirt, black pants under a black apron. A brass name tag worn close to her left breast spelled out the name in block letters. . . .

"Silvia."

"Excuse me?" she said.

Heller blinked twice. "What?"

"Would you like to see a menu?"

It was the same question she always asked.

"Just coffee."

"Coffee . . ."

"Coffee," Heller repeated.

"I know," she said. "It'll be a minute."

Heller nodded, trying to think of a way to take the conversation past a simple exchange between customer and waitress. He had been trying for over six months, and today the result was no different. He was still nodding when she turned her back and left him alone at his table.

Silvia walked over to the counter. The coffeepot was brewing, slowly filling, drop by drop. She leaned against the stereo, folded her arms, tapped a pen against her elbows, patiently watched the coffee creep to the top of the pot.

Heller watched her out of the corner of his eye. He pretended to be engrossed in an autographed picture of Sarah

Jessica Parker hanging on a nearby wall. He watched Silvia stare into that coffeepot, wondered how someone so small and frail looking could possibly be one year his senior. Watched Silvia, kept his eyes as close to her as he could. Heller knew that any moment now she would bring that pen to her lips and give it a slight nibble. It was Heller's favorite moment of each day.

There it was.

She nibbled with her top set of teeth, kept her lower lip tucked over the bottom set. Concentration. Heller knew that expression by heart. Traced it every night in his mind before he went to sleep. She had the kind of eyes that made Heller want to crawl inside her soul, fall asleep there so he could catch a glimpse of her dreams before sunlight scared them away.

"You were right, bike boy."

Heller tore himself away from Silvia.

Sitting at his table was a Haitian man with close-cropped hair and a brown leather vest, smiling so widely you would have thought he'd won the lottery.

"Two weeks later," the Haitian told him. "Two weeks later and I've met the most fantastic woman. She even speaks French, man. Educated, too . . ."

Heller looked around, thought he might find an answer at a nearby table. When nothing surfaced, he looked helplessly at his new friend, tried his best to seem understanding.

The Haitian saw Heller was drawing a blank, laughed. "Christoph Toussaint. Remember me? You brought me the news about my woman in Haiti. I wasn't planning on killing myself, I was just talking a lot of talk. Man talk. You know how a woman can make a man weak in the knees, especially when she is taken away, but . . . it turns out you were right. Two weeks after you told me about the death of my girlfriend, luck smiled on me again. Did I mention she speaks French?"

Before Heller could answer, Silvia was at their table again. She placed a saucer in front of Heller, a spoon for stirring.

"Cream or sugar?" she asked.

"Yes," Heller answered.

"Both?"

"Creamy."

"Cream," Silvia said, about to turn when Christoph took hold of her arm, stopped her.

"Yes, dear," he said, charm radiating from his smile. "I would like just a cup of hot water, please."

"Just hot water?"

"Yes," he explained, pulling a silver case out of his pocket. "I bring my own herbs with me, specially grown by my mother. You can charge me the price of a tea—I don't mind, darling."

She nodded, made a note in her pad.

"You really are something else, girl," he said, beaming. "Look at you. You have such fine, dark hair. . . ."

Silvia looked embarrassed, but she smiled nonetheless, and it may have been genuine.

"And those eyes. I promise you, you must turn the head of *every* man in this place. Tell me I'm right." Christoph turned to Heller. "Isn't she something?"

Heller couldn't bring himself to conjure a simple nod.

"Just water?" Silvia asked again.

"Just water, beautiful," Christoph said.

Silvia walked back behind the counter. Heller kept close watch on her as she filled a cup with hot water. Some of the steam drifted into her face, left beads of precipitation resting there. Silvia picked up a napkin, wiped her cheeks free of water. Her shirt lifted slightly, exposing her belly button.

Round stomach.

Heller felt his own stomach turn with a painful glee.

"She's a beautiful girl."

Heller's attention snapped back to Christoph. "What?"

"She was a beautiful girl," Christoph said, "but it's amazing how fast things can make themselves better. . . . Death can be so strange. You know?"

Heller felt a sudden pressure in his head. "I know . . ."

"Ah, well, you're young," Christoph said. "There is so much left for you to discover."

Silvia returned with the cream and hot water. She didn't stay any longer than she needed to, just walked over to her next table. There wasn't much joy or enthusiasm, just something Heller couldn't escape—her ability to *continue*. . . .

"When I first started coming here, she was working in the kitchen," Heller said, suddenly aware he was talking. "She worked in the kitchen. You'd hardly catch a glimpse of her. . . . Now she's here. Now she's here, and look at how great she's doing. . . ."

Christoph showed approval for all things with his smile.

Heller bit his lip and reached for the cream.

He was about to pour it in his coffee when he noticed a string hanging out of his cup. He pulled at it, lifted a tea bag up from its depths. Drops of water dripped down from the end, rhythmically. He stared at it.

"Oh, hey, man," Christoph said, "if I had known you were asking for tea, I would have let you have some of my herbs. Much better than anything that comes in a bag. You should come to my place sometime. My woman will cook for the both of us. First woman I've met in this country who can actually cook plantains . . ."

Heller nodded, put the tea bag back in his cup.

He picked up the cream and started to pour.

chapter seven

Heller's grandmother, Florence, cooked that night.

Reheated. Leftovers from the previous evening, Heller's birthday. Jerk chicken with beans and rice. It was a recipe Heller's mother had picked up when they were in Jamaica five or six years ago, and then passed on to Florence, who from that day always referred to the recipe as *Chicken à la daughter-in-law*.

It had been Heller's favorite meal for ages.

The three of them sat in the kitchen with their dinner. Heller ate mechanically, could feel his grandparents' silent questions. It was difficult. There was no easy way for him to tell them how his day had gone, and there was no easy way for them to respond to his silence. Conversation made out of the sound of silverware and chewing. It was toward the end of the meal when Florence finally said, "Your parents called today."

Heller looked up from his food, interested, worried.

"They were sad to have missed you. . . . They say things are going fine, they said. The health community center is already up—not quite flourishing, but still. . . . The villagers can pay for the medicine, but it's just not arriving on time. They have running water now, and the situation seems to be improving. . . ." She put down her fork and knife, looked to her husband.

"I think they wanted you to know that," Eric finished, wiping his mouth.

Heller looked at the two of them, knew there was something expected of him. "I'm glad," he said. "I'm glad they've managed to do what they've done."

After a moment of nothing, Florence stood, picked up the plates, and carried them over to the sink. Heller watched his grandfather take care of the glasses, and then he wiped the table.

"There's still cake left over from yesterday," Florence said. "Would you like some, dear?"

"Sure," Heller answered, tossing the rag into the sink. "I just need to go to my room and take care of a few things."

His grandparents both nodded.

"Okay," Heller said.

Heller closed the door behind him.

His desk faced a wall. The only other furnishings in the room were his bed, a closet, a nightstand, and a pair of bookshelves. All along the wall were posters of bicycles and cyclists. His shelves were lined with model bikes, toy bikes, and photographs of bike races. The light was soft, and the decorations all blended together.

Heller walked over to his closet, opened the door.

His clothes greeted him, and nestled between a large box and a pile of laundry was a pair of Rollerblades. He stared them down, defiant, muttering threats under his breath. The Rollerblades did nothing, but their silence was enough to encourage Heller to slam the door, walk over to his desk.

Heller sat himself down and pulled at one of the drawers. He took out a folder. Plain, manila, with the words GRAND TOUR scrawled on the cover in black marker. He opened it. Inside were pages and pages of printouts, detailed figures scrawled and summed to the decimal point.

Heller checked to make sure his door was closed, remembered that it was, and pulled out his paycheck. He took a look at his earnings for the last two weeks, made a quick note on a slip of paper, and carefully marked the date for 07/05/01. He put the note aside, sifted through the sheets of paper. He stopped. Columns of numbers, addition after addition after addition, totaling up to a number in the early thousands . . .

He made a final count of his estimates, closed the folder, returned it to its bed, closed the drawer. Heller stared into space for a while, another day gone by. He got up, walked to his bed, lay on his back, bathed in the glow of his posters and bedside lamp. "I'm coming to get you," Heller whispered to the ceiling. "I'm coming to get you, Henri Cornet. . . ."

Heller heard his grandmother calling from the kitchen—something about cake, something about dessert. He let the sound drain out of the world, arms behind his head, lost in other thoughts.

"I'm coming to get you, Henri Cornet. . . ."

Heller closed his eyes for a moment, only to find, moments later, that hours had passed, and it was now time to get back to work.

chapter eight

The morning rush was over and the office was losing steam.

Heller stood at Iggy's desk. A few of the other staff members wandered in and out, some already packing up for the day. News never fit any sort of pattern at Soft Tidings. It always seemed to be happening, waning, flaring up, fading, and never in any particular order. Events emerged, disappeared, and it was up to anybody within arm's reach to make any sort of sense out of it.

"We got one for you," Iggy told Heller. "You listening?"

"Yeah."

"Hold on." Iggy picked up the phone on his desk, punched a button, and kicked his voice up an octave. "Soft Tidings, news with a personal touch . . . All right . . . Sam Myer . . . What . . . ? If he works for you, then where can we find him . . . ?" Iggy reached for a pen and began scribbling. "All right . . . of course . . . sure."

Iggy gave a silent nod into the phone, turned to Heller.

"All right, you got two. The first one is for Salim Adasi, Lower East Side address. Turkish man, bad break from back home. It's from his sister—not urgent, so you can take your time on this one, if that's possible for you."

"Who was that on the phone?" Heller asked.

"This is complicated." Iggy scratched the back of his head with a pen. "I don't think we've ever had anything quite like this before. In fact, I question whether or not we should even be doing it."

Heller's pulse quickened. "What is it?"

Iggy hesitated. He glanced behind him, toward Dimitri's office. The door was closed, locked possibly. Iggy looked back up at Heller, sighed. "All right . . ."

Heller leaned forward, curious, eager.

"All right," Iggy repeated. He glanced back to Dimitri's office for one last time before looking Heller in the eye. "I guess you're our guinea pig, Heller. You up for this?"

Heller nodded.

Iggy sighed. "His name is Sam Myer. You can find him at a discount store down on Canal. They told me it's his second job. . . ."

Iggy gave him the details.

Heller leaned against the wall of the storage room. Sam Myer sat on a box among many, most stacked against the wall and up to the ceiling. A single fluorescent light lit the dirty walls. Neither of them had spoken for five minutes. Sam looked defeated. Elbows on his knees, head resting on his hands, staring at nothing. When he first saw him, Heller had pegged Sam at thirty-four, thirty-five. Over the course of their conversation he had aged, and Heller slowly noticed a gray hair in the forest of black, crow's feet adorning tired eyes.

"So this is how they tell me . . . ," Sam murmured. He looked up, right at Heller. "After five years, they let me go with a telegram."

Heller shifted his position.

"Foreign labor, that's what it is," Sam continued, anger barely held in check. "Cheap foreign labor—how the hell am I supposed to compete with that?"

"You still have this job . . . ," Heller ventured.

"This is Christmas money!" Sam yelled, steadied himself. "I do this to earn that little extra so I can get my kids toys, good clothes so they don't have to go to school looking like a thrift-store purchase. My kids eat, they eat food. They live in a cramped apartment, but at least there's a ceiling and electricity so they can do their homework after dark. Christmas money's not gonna give them any of that. . . ."

Heller didn't know what to say.

"And they think telling me through a telegram makes it better."

"It's not a telegram, it's a personalized message," Heller corrected.

"It's all the same to me—they still didn't have the stones to say this to my face." Sam shrugged, stood up. "What am I supposed to do now?"

The door to the storage room opened. A boy of twenty-something with green highlights in his hair poked his head in. "Sam, you going to be much longer?" He wore a name tag reading: MANAGER.

"I'll be out in a bit," Sam answered.

The door closed. Heller was left alone with the man.

Heller thought about it. Then began with, "Just yesterday, I delivered a message to a Chinese woman whose son had died in a reeducation camp. . . ."

He relayed the story, the events of his visit with Mrs. Chiang. He described the apartment, the figurines, the wooden horse with the crippled butterfly carved into its belly. Heller told the story as it was—didn't know why, but it was something he did when all else failed on his visits. Sometimes a connection could be made.

When he was done, Heller gave Sam the chance to think about it.

It didn't take Sam very long: "Why did you tell me that?"

"Perspective, I guess."

"Perspective?" Sam laughed, only it came out choked, a coughing sound that rattled in the barren room. "Perspective from a teenager. You know what? We sell those little wooden horses at this store. I get a minimum wage selling those little bastards, but at least it's something. And now it looks like it's all I have. So don't talk to me about perspective, who makes what and for what wages. I have a wife and two kids, I don't have *time* for perspective. I don't have room for perspective in my life when some suit decides to fire me so he can hire someone for a few dollars less—"

"You don't know why you got fired."

"And neither do you." Sam was trembling, his muscles taut. "You don't know anything about me, so don't tell me how I need to feel."

"You're being unfair."

"So is everyone else."

The door to the storage room opened again, and the manager-boy made his second appearance.

"Hey, Sam, you coming back?"

"I'LL BE THERE!" Sam yelled.

"Hey—" The manager's voice sounded soothing under the glow of the light. "Take your time, man. Take your time."

Sam turned to Heller.

"Anything else?"

Heller recognized Sam's expression. It was meant to make him feel young. Inexperienced. Ignorant. Heller was familiar with the look; most kids his age were. It was part of life, growing up, but it was also part of his job. And when he was on the job, that look never once found its mark.

"Mr. Myer," Heller began. "What's your wife's name?"

"Angela."

"Been married long?"

"Twelve years."

"First marriage?"

"Yeah."

"That's good. For the kids especially. Things are complicated enough."

Sam agreed silently.

"Twelve years . . . ," Heller mused. "You've been married to Angela since I was four. Since before I could make a sentence with my hands . . . You love her still?"

"Of course."

"She still love you?"

Sam sat back down, sank into a box marked FRAGILE. "She tells me every night."

"Well." Heller chose his words carefully. "I'm only sixteen. So I don't know what that's like. . . . It sounds nice, Mr. Myer."

Sam kept his eyes to the floor.

"Anything else?" Heller asked.

Sam shook his head.

Heller walked out of the room, through the metal door and into the store. Useless trinkets and tiny gadgets filling every corner. He walked down a few aisles, stopped at a basket filled with little wooden horses.

Picked one up. Looked underneath, saw a half butterfly carved into its stomach.

Picked up another one, looked underneath.

The same.

He repeated the process five or six times, each time resulting in the same conclusion. A customer walked past, picked up his own horse, examined it. Took it to the counter and paid his dollar.

Heller thought about it, stared down at the horses, watched them stare back at him. All those eyes, those half-dead butterflies, countless messages of hope for Mrs. Chiang. There seemed to be little basis for it. It was either a message or a generic stamp. Half a butterfly, fifty-fifty. Not much of a bet. Not much to be sure of.

Heller glanced to the back of the store.

Sam was standing there, steadfast at the entrance to the storage room.

Their eyes met.

Sam nodded.

Heller put down the horse and left the store as quickly as he could.

chapter nine

Heller knew at once that the two men who answered the door were recent immigrants to New York. From somewhere in the Middle East, he guessed, though he didn't want to make any further assumption; Heller found it wasn't good for his work. The two men seemed nervous, keeping the door open just enough to let their eyes peer out.

"Is Mr. Salim Adasi in?" Heller asked.

"No, no," one of them said, a strong accent nearly drowning his words. "He works right now."

"Do you know where he works?"

The two looked at each other quickly, then the second man answered, "He commutes."

"He will be back later," the first man added.

"In an hour, two hours," the second specified.

"All right," Heller said. "I'll be back later, then. Good—"

They closed the door without so much as a nod in Heller's direction. Heller glanced up and down the vacant hallway, its walls hotter than the outside world. He smacked his lips, heard the sound resonate in the space around him.

He went down the warped steps and pressed warily against the front door.

It swung open with ease.

Held open by a man with a light dent in his left cheek, a mark resembling a soft scar.

Heller gave a polite, automatic nod in the man's direction and headed for his bike.

The man went in, closed the door, and looked through the glass with familiar interest as Heller unchained his bike.

Heller glanced back to the door of the apartment building, sensing something in the overbearing warmth around him. Sunlight refracted off the window in the door, a white, blinding glare. Heller squeezed his eyes shut, spots dancing from the bright beam of illumination.

He opened them, shook his head.

Heller had a few hours to kill, and though he *really* did not feel like having a cup of coffee, he knew just where he was going nonetheless.

chapter ten

Heller was watching her write out a bill when he noticed her hands begin to shake. He could tell even from across the room, and he paused, cup against his lips, coffee trickling slowly into his mouth.

Silvia's hands were shaking. It was slight, her pen paused in midarithmetic, unable to finish writing a three, or possibly an eight. Everyone else kept on with their books and unpublished manuscripts, same as any other day, while Heller kept watching Silvia's throat contract slightly, eyes shimmering. She bit her lower lip. Heller watched a tear make its way down her cheek and into her mouth.

Heller tried to bite his own lip, and coffee spilled down his chin and into his lap. He put down his cup, too quickly. It made a loud cracking sound against the table and a dozen heads shot up. Heller mumbled an apology to himself, still dribbling coffee. He searched for a napkin, came up short. From the table next to him an empathetic cough. A fat man with painted fingernails offered him a napkin. Heller accepted and mumbled a second apology.

"Thank *you*," the fat man said.

Heller was unsure if he had heard correctly.

"Thank you for your message last month," the fat man said, voice so low it scraped the floor. "You helped me a lot. . . ."

Heller always had trouble recognizing his past customers outside their apartments and could never find words that suited any other situation. He mumbled again, wiped the coffee from his face, off his lap. Heller looked up to see if Silvia had noticed.

Silvia was gone.

Heller blinked, then looked around. Through the window, he caught sight of her, rummaging through a small black purse. She was still in her work clothes: red shirt and black jeans, sandals on her feet. Heller watched her glance around as though getting her bearings. Strands of hair stuck to her face. She paused, thinking.

Heller absently placed a five-dollar bill on the table, rose to his feet, walked to the door, wondering what might happen if he brushed her hair aside with his fingers, asked why she was crying. His steps were cautious, mind barely convinced of what he planned to do, breath short.

If I asked you what was wrong and you told me, maybe I could let you know a few things about me. Maybe I could stop talking to your name tag and form words beyond "coffee" and "check, please." Maybe we both could . . .

The world seemed to be going in slow motion. As it turned out, it was only Heller. By the time he made it out the door, Silvia was already halfway down Prince Street.

The blast of heat almost knocked Heller over. Still determined to do something, though not entirely sure what, he freed his bike from its hitching post and followed on foot.

Silvia turned north on Sixth Avenue. Heller remained twenty feet behind, watching her walk, his hands on the bike's handlebars. The chain made barely audible clicking noises, and Heller glanced around nervously, wondering if people on the street would see what he was up to, grow suspicious of him. Petrified at the thought of his grandfather happening past, catching Heller in his lie.

The day had turned gray. Overcast skies breathed life into the clouds. Not a gust of wind in the air. Thick humidity turned the streets into swamps. An A/C/E train passed below, underground, its rumble like thunder.

Tired faces walked by, all lost to Heller in the movement of Silvia's hips. He couldn't even take the time to wander, take note of his surroundings, the gentle but abrupt change of traffic lights.

The sudden screech of tires.

"Watch it, IDIOT!"

Heller snapped to sudden attention.

Middle of the street, a car's bumper resting inches from his bike. The driver was a young man with slicked-back hair, expensive sunglasses wrapped around his face. He had sharp Italian features. Heller watched him bounce his head to bass-filled music, lyrics screaming guns, drugs, and money. Neither recognized the other from their encounter the previous day, when Heller had grabbed onto the young Italian's car in the name of speed.

The horn blared. Heller coughed, managed an embarrassed:

"Sorry, man, s'okay . . ."

. . . before checking to see if Silvia had noticed him.

She hadn't, same as any other day.

Heller walked on, face eight shades of crimson.

Silvia walked into a drugstore. Heller parked himself on a bench across the way. Father Demo Square was sparsely settled that day. More pigeons than people, both of which moved with a certain slowness. Heller bought a bagel from a passing vendor. He sat and kept watch between bites of poppy seed.

Another rumble from the subway, farther away, echoing past Heller's ears.

A hand fell on his shoulder. Heller jumped, turned. A Jamaican man with a thick forest of dreadlocks and a beard stood behind him, looking down. In his other hand was an umbrella.

"Only three dollars, my friend."

Heller finished the bite in his mouth, swallowed. "For the umbrella?"

"Three dollars."

"It's not raining."

"Do you know which way the wind is blowing?"

Heller shook his head.

"From the east . . ." The man's voice was soft, almost pristine. "The east winds are blowing, and the clouds are gathering. Four dollars and you can take a second one home to your girl."

"No." Heller thought about it. "No thanks."

"All right, man. Take care."

The Jamaican continued down his path. Heller saw him amble along, then disappear around a corner. He looked back out across the street.

Heller froze.

Silvia was standing in the middle of Father Demo Square. No more than ten feet away. She was inspecting a package of photographs, leafing through pictures with slow deliberation. Heller didn't move, still shocked at her proximity, trying to stop himself from instinctively reaching for a cup of coffee that wasn't there. Silvia paused, scratched her nose. A pigeon hopped onto Heller's bench and started eating his bagel. The day grew more humid, somehow.

Heller couldn't take his eyes off her.

Silvia lifted her head.

Lifted her head and looked right at Heller.

And Heller thought his entire life might end in that one moment. Eyes ensnared, a connection so strong it turned the city inside out. It was like riding a bike. Pedaling through midmorning traffic with nothing but the pavement to see him safe. Same sensation. Same rush. Same beautiful taste of certainty.

Heller felt he could lose himself in her stare.

She gave him a smile that reminded him of a memory he'd never experienced.

Heller gave her the same smile.

Only she didn't recognize it.

She wasn't even looking at him.

Looking past him, that's what it was.

Past him, through him, into some other time and place where things were different.

It was a place Heller wanted to be.

It was a place Heller had yet to find.

The subway rumbled again, and the sound bled out of the sky.

Silvia closed her bag, heading east.

Heller tossed his bagel to the birds and stood up.

He followed her to a post office alongside the Citibank on LaGuardia. She went inside. Heller checked his watch. He still had that one last delivery to make. He waited. People wandered out of the bank, most on cell phones, some filtering into the post office.

Heller felt he was on the edge of a decision, needed something, a push.

A sign.

"Well, goddamn!" came the voice behind him. "I will be goddamned—the stallion finally got off the horse."

Heller's eyes grew wide, deer in a set of headlights.

Bruno the Bruiser was standing in front of him, the balance of power always on his side, face ready, anticipating an excuse to act.

"Looks like our complaints got you grounded, you little bastard."

Heller couldn't bring himself to speak.

"Let me ask you this, Highland: What does it mean?"

Heller stammered, "I don't know what—"

"To the GRAND TOUR!" Bruno yelled, mocking, eyes malevolent. A few people on the street turned their faces, avoiding the scene. "What the hell does it mean, anyway?"

"It means . . . I have to go."

"Yeah, who died?"

"I need to . . . buy some stamps."

Heller walked toward the entrance of the post office.

"What you need to buy is a pair of ROLLERBLADES!" Bruno yelled.

Heller chained his bike and let the door to the post office close behind him. He was dismayed to find that the customer service area occupied less space than his room, leaving him few places to remain unnoticed. Silvia was standing in line for the stamp machine.

Casual, Heller thought desperately and stood in line, directly behind Silvia. Stood with stiff posture, staring at the back of her head, that luminous, dark hair. The line progressed at a steady clip, and Heller moved along, not entirely sure what he was hoping to accomplish. People lined up behind him. He felt trapped between the important and the incidental.

Silvia made it to the stamp machine. Heller watched her pull out a wrinkled dollar bill, corners folded over. She inserted it into the slot. Machinery whirred, sucked in the dollar bill, vomited the money back out. Silvia tried again with the same results.

She repeated this.

Several times.

The line grew annoyed, mumbles from the rest clearly intended for Silvia to hear. Heller saw her hands begin to shake. He reached into his pocket, felt for change. He stepped out of line, held the handful of change out for her. Silvia didn't notice, tears of frustration in her eyes, hands still trembling. Heller couldn't speak and his hands started to quiver. Both of them standing there, hands trembling until finally, from the back of the line:

"JUST GIVE HER THE COINS, YOU MORON!"

Silvia jumped with surprise, whirled, knocked the coins out of Heller's hands, dropped her photographs onto the floor along with the change.

They both bent down to the ground, faces flushed. In his scramble to pick up the quarters, Heller scattered Silvia's pictures even more. The silver faces of George Washington seemed to betray a mild amusement.

"Coins," Heller managed.

"What?"

"Use the coins."

Heller pointed to the stamp machine. Silvia understood. She took the coins, got up, and started feeding them into the slot.

Heller was about to stand when he spied a photograph lying a few feet away, forgotten. He glanced up, saw Silvia trying to decide on her stamps. Without thinking, before he could even consider his actions, Heller scooped up the photograph in one deft motion and pocketed it.

He stood as Silvia retrieved her stamps. She thanked him distractedly and handed him her dollar, walked right past him, out the door.

The bell above the frame jingled goodbye.

Heller blinked, looked down at the dollar bill. Washington again. That amused expression had become a wry smile. Heller stuffed the dollar into his pocket and chased after Silvia.

There was no need to go very far. She was standing next to Heller's bike, trying to put her photographs away. Heller walked up to her. A tear was caught in midstride down her cheek.

"Are you an actress?" Heller blurted out.

Silvia looked completely confused.

". . . Or a model," Heller continued. "Sorry, you could be a model; it's just that I saw those photographs and it made me wonder . . . wonder if you were a model . . . or an actress."

Silvia didn't answer immediately. It started to rain, a faint drizzle enveloping the air. Her eyes were damp, and Heller was about to repeat his question when she said, "They're for my father."

"Where's your father?"

"At home, in Chile . . ." It was as though she were talking to herself, through the tears, and out into the world in general. "If my mother ever finds out I'm sending him anything, I don't know what she'll do, but he hasn't heard from me in two years and . . . and I don't care if he's a *perdido*. Would you care if your father was a *perdido*? Because I don't care what he did or who he did it to!"

The rain had grown heavier.

"My father's not a . . ." Heller searched for words. "But, then again, I haven't seen my father in—"

Silvia cut him off with an abrupt "Damn it!" Her photographs had gotten wet and she hurried them back into her purse.

"Thanks for the coins," she told him. Silvia looked up to the ashen skies, let the water run down her face, skin glistening. "Now I can't even tell if I'm crying anymore. . . ."

There was hardly time to process Silvia's words before she ran off, down the sidewalk, puddles shattering under her sandals. Heller watched her grow smaller. Stood in the downpour, getting soaked as the city silently thanked the sky.

A gale of laughter reached Heller's ears. He looked across the street. There, standing on the curb, was the Jamaican umbrella salesman. His arms were extended, a smile on his face that made Heller forget the rest of the world, if only for an instant.

"Just sold my last two, man!" He laughed, and the sound echoed in the alleyways. "From the east, my friend, from the east!"

The Jamaican's call was answered by the bark of authority:

"Keep that noise DOWN!"

Heller and the Jamaican both turned to see Bruno standing on an adjacent corner.

"What!?" the Jamaican yelled across the block.

"Keep that noise down!"

"I can't stop the rain, man!"

The Jamaican and Bruno broke out in an argument that filled the streets, washed into the gutters along with the rain. Heller looked at his watch; the digital numbers told him he had fallen behind schedule on his last delivery and it was time.

With thoughts of Silvia and a planet falling from grace drilling into his mind, Heller unchained his bike, jumped on, ready to let it all melt away.

With a terrific shout, Heller dashed into the streets. He took a sharp left on his handlebars, rode right past Bruno with enough speed to send a tidal wave of water onto his uniform.

"GRAND TOUR!" Heller belted out, pedaled in a southbound direction, far from Silvia and the clash of conflict. He moved on, waiting for the right crossroad to present itself in a stoplight moment.

But the rain had arrived and the city was cooling down. For a while . . .

chapter eleven

His tires screeched to a halt in front of a Lower East Side apartment.

Got off his bike, hit the button on his watch, checked his time.

"Thirteen twenty. Damn."

Heller made his way up the same warped staircase and found himself confronted with the same pair of Middle Eastern men walking down and out onto the streets.

"Salim is home now if you want to see him."

Heller thanked them, continued up the steps, face set with a grim determination.

Found the apartment.

Knocked on the door.

Checked his card, got the information straight.

The door opened.

Standing there was the man who had held the door to the apartment building open for Heller earlier. Heller recognized him immediately and saw what might have been a similar familiarity in the man's expression. A deeper familiarity, perhaps, like catching a glimpse of an old friend in a strange crowd years later.

"Mr. Salim Adasi?" Heller asked.

"Yes . . ." His accent was a light Turkish hue, voice relaxed. "And you are the bike boy."

"Well . . ." Heller didn't know how Salim could have known that. "I'm more of a messenger."

"What kind of messenger?" Salim asked with a near childlike curiosity.

"Soft Tidings," Heller said.

Salim's eyebrows furrowed slightly. "What does that mean?"

"Well, it's news . . . with a personal touch."

"Ah." Salim's eyes lit up. "Come in, come in. We are all in much need of some good news from home."

They walked into the apartment together. Their footsteps made shuffling noises on the concrete floor. The walls were an empty sort of yellow, free of decoration, except for the occasional chip or spiderweb cracks. Five cots dotted the room. Stacks and stacks of books filled the remaining space, all piled low. Gray daylight filtered through the windows, spotlight on dancing dust.

"Have a seat," Salim said, a warmth in his eyes that took Heller a few moments to get used to.

Heller sat on a nearby cot. Sat on something lying on the cot, something that groaned, muttered an unintelligible protest. He shot up, looked down. A man was lying there, covered entirely by an old blanket. Heller's heart was in his throat. He glanced at Salim Adasi.

"Have another seat," Salim said. "Take a chair."

Heller looked around. He realized that the stacks of

books had been arranged around the room as a replacement for furniture. He could almost make out a chair, a table, a nightstand.

Salim motioned with his hand.

Heller followed Salim's directions to a pile of books. He sat down, felt the pages compress underneath him.

Salim sat on his own pile of dog-eared literature. He rubbed his hands together, placed them on his knees. "So, who sent you?" he asked. "My mother? Or was it my sister? Is she finally going to have a baby?"

"It is from your sister. But it's not about a baby. It's not about anybody's baby. . . . It's about Nizima."

Salim's face flooded with hope. "So, Nizima—she is coming then?"

"I don't think so. . . . Your sister says she's going to marry someone else. . . . She says you'll know who."

Heller watched as Salim's eyes changed. Changed focus, softened. Heller watched, waiting. Waiting because he knew it was always the others who spoke first, and it was in those moments where Heller found his own words.

Salim didn't say anything.

Heller didn't recognize the look in Salim's eyes, tried to think if he had seen anything like it before. It was as though Salim wasn't so much letting the news soak in as asking it to soak in.

All the while saying nothing.

Heller watched Salim's features speak in some invisible tongue, tried to guess at how long silence could last.

One story up, a floorboard creaked.

Heller cleared his throat.

"Mr. Adasi, I—"

"The swelling of the rose geranium," Salim began. His voice was calm, a red shade of understanding.

"The humming of the sea,
and fall is here with its full clouds and wise earth . . .
my love,
the years have ripened.
We've gone through so much
We could be a thousand years old.
But we are still
Wide-eyed children
Running barefoot in the sand, hand in hand."
Heller spoke instantly, without thinking:
"Mr. Adasi, if—"
"We could be a thousand years old," Salim repeated. He paused, thinking. Then: "That was written by Nazim Hikmet, one of the greatest Turkish poets to ever walk this earth. He spent most of his life in prison and in exile . . . and you may call me Salim. . . ."

A sleepy second elapsed before a groan from one of the cots reached Heller's ear. The slumbering man threw his feet onto the ground, stood, stretched, barely acknowledging Heller and Salim. He crossed between them as he walked into the bathroom. No sound apart from his movements, then the slightly audible sound of pissing through the paper-thin walls.

Salim leaned over, face close to Heller's. "They would think I was mad to still be in love with a woman promised to another man since before she was born. . . ." Salim's eyes pointed to the other room, and he put a finger to his lips. "There are things they don't know."

The bathroom door swung open, the man retracing his

steps back to his cot. He collapsed, hitting the pillow with a weight that far exceeded his body. He was asleep before his first breath left his lungs.

"You have brought me great news . . . ," Salim said, voice returning to room temperature. "This . . . is wonderful."

Heller was at a loss. "I know my job, Salim. I can promise you this is *not* good news. I don't deliver good news . . . it's not what I do."

Salim contemplated Heller with an ambiguous smile. Heller tried to smile back, do something, succeeded only in biting his lip.

"How old are you?" Salim asked.

"Sixteen."

Salim nodded. He reached over and mussed Heller's hair; reached down, rubbed his hand against the stack of books pretending to be a chair and then against Heller's face; let the dust and grime collect on his cheeks, temples, and forehead. Heller remained still through all of it, slowly growing aware that the drumbeat of rain had fallen silent against the windows.

Salim sat back as he studied Heller with a critical eye.

He smiled. "Now you look twenty-one. Let's go down to the bar."

Heller went over to the window, where his face was suddenly visible. He checked the reflection, saw that he did, in fact, look older.

Heller breathed in, took in an assault of dust.

He sneezed.

chapter twelve

Heller kept telling himself that it was his last delivery of the day. So he wouldn't have to report to work until morning. So there were no further obligations weighing him down. So this was why he was following Salim into the heart of the Village.

Freedom from responsibility.

Spare time.

The three of them walked side by side by side. Salim, Heller, and his bike. Salim ambled with a slow, steady stride. Reliable. Predictable, and yet Heller had trouble matching his own steps to the Turk's. Heller was silent, unsure if he was still a representative of Soft Tidings or if he had already clocked out. Standing on a line he was unfamiliar with.

Walking with an unfamiliar man down familiar city streets.

Salim wasn't quick to open his mouth, either. Every now and again he would ask a question, tell Heller something, never in any rush for a response.

"Are you from the city, Heller?"

"I've lived here most of my life."

A few blocks later: "Have you ever been to Turkey?"

"No."

"Oh, it's such a place. . . . Something about it, you know? Home."

Next thing, he was pointing to an alcove between two buildings. "That is where I used to set up my book stand. I must have spent every day there for three months before I was usurped. Usurped by students setting up a table to collect money for the homeless. I have not found a spot quite like it. . . ."

"It's a nice spot."

"It was. . . ."

It wasn't long before Heller noticed something. It had been gnawing at his mind for several minutes before it finally hit him. Salim wouldn't speak unless they were standing at a crosswalk. Waiting for the lights to change at an intersection. Other than that, their walk was composed purely of city sounds.

Once Heller picked up on it, he found himself becoming a part of it. "How long have you been in New York, Salim?"

"A year."

"You speak English well."

"I learned in Istanbul. You have to know English these days; it is necessary."

Heller was amused by the pace of the conversation. He gave it another go at the next intersection:

"I don't speak Turkish."

"Do you speak Kurdish?"

"No . . ."

It was Salim's turn to look amused. "Of course not."

During their trek from the Lower East Side the sun had begun its descent. They were walking up LaGuardia now, pausing at the intersection on Houston Street. The rush of a thousand cars added to the light breeze brought by the rainstorm.

"Do you like living in America?" Heller asked.

Salim didn't answer. They made their way up another block, then stopped.

Heller looked up at Salim, saw his eyes lost in the twilight. All around them, nightlife was appearing out of the brightly lit doorways, rising with the steam from the streets.

"You can never call a place home until you have buried someone there," Salim told Heller. "The prophet Muhammad never said he was going to return from the dead. He knew it wasn't necessary. . . . So what comes next?" Salim's eyes were distant. "You wander. Keep wandering. You wander until you find the place you can call home. It is easy for a Muslim to forget this." He paused, waiting for the traffic light to grant them safety. "It is easy for anyone to forget this. . . ."

The DON'T WALK sign changed its mind and the two of them crossed the street, taking a westbound direction on Bleecker. Piercing parlors, jazz clubs, and pizza for a dollar seventy-five a slice.

"If you're a Muslim," Heller ventured, aware that they were midway along a city block, "then how come we're going to a bar?"

Salim waited until they had reached the corner of Bleecker and MacDougal Street, where he paused, thinking.

"I never drink," he said in a way that made Heller think

that there was more to it than that. "But a Kurdish wedding lasts several days. . . . I think God will understand."

"Will he?"

Salim nodded.

Traffic continued on its due course.

chapter thirteen

The stairs had led them underground, into a bar called Creole Nights.

No more than ten steps, but Heller couldn't help but feel he'd entered another world. Still New York. Only smaller.

A tiny dive.

Not cramped. Comfortable.

The walls were a dirty yellow, cracks displaying what must have once been a semiwhite sort of color underneath. Candles lit the room, backed by the soft orange glow of scattered lamps built into the bar. The tables were rickety, chairs the same. Stapled to the ceiling were rows and rows of straw hats hung upside down. A tabby cat prowled around underfoot on a smooth, red-brick floor dotted with cigarette burns.

It was early. A pair of waitresses at the far end slicing lemons, a few Haitian men sitting, talking shop with the bartender. In a far corner, some musicians were setting up their instruments, comparing sheet music.

Everyone greeted Salim as he walked in, like an old

friend back from battle. He threw his arms up, a warm embrace for the entire group. Walked right over to the bar, shook hands, kissed the waitresses, the bartender. He laughed along with everyone else and returned a smile for each one given to him.

It was warm down there. Genuinely warm.

Heller stood by the door, awkward, taking everything in, curious and unsure. He glanced behind him, back up the stairs, making sure his bike was still chained to the tree outside. Making sure the city was still there, that he hadn't fallen down a rabbit hole. Heller shifted his weight from one foot to another, crossed his arms, uncrossed them.

Reggae music poured softly from the speakers.

One of the waitresses, a blonde with intense blue eyes and round, elfin features, walked briskly across the room. Black pants, a belt adorned with metal studs. Black shirt, a figure impossible to ignore; Heller was still trying to when she got to him, soft smile and pleasant smoker's voice.

"Would you like to sit?"

"I'm with Salim," Heller said, too shy to look at her. "I came in with him."

"Oh, Salim . . . ," she said, as though Heller had cracked some sort of code. "I'll just put you at his usual table."

The waitress led him to a round table. Heller sat with his back to a large mural depicting a crowd of people gathered in a Caribbean village. The waitress handed him a drink menu. Pulled a pen out of her hair.

"What can I get you?"

Heller stared at the list of drinks, felt like he was reading Latin. Panicked, he pointed randomly and plunged ahead:

"How's the melon ball?"

"You don't want that."

"I don't?"

"Nobody wants that—it's like drinking syrup."

"Well . . . what do I want?"

"You want a Jack Daniel's," she told him, sounding incredibly sure of herself.

"He wants a ginger ale," Salim informed them, sitting down at the table with a wry smile. "I don't want you corrupting my friend with your Tennessee poison."

"It's not poison," she insisted. "It's sunshine."

"Just get the boy a ginger ale and a double gin and tonic for me."

"Nope."

"Please, my dear?"

"No."

"Must I beg?" Salim put his hands together, eyes of a lost dog.

The waitress smiled slyly, winked at Heller, and went back to the bar.

Salim laughed and turned to Heller. "That's Wanda. She is from Kentucky. Wanda writes her own poetry, wonderful poetry. She has such a spirit about her, don't you think?"

"She's beautiful," Heller said, before realizing the words were coming. He closed his mouth, bit his lip, tried to reverse time by adding, "I mean she's . . . astute."

"Astute, beautiful . . ." Salim shifted in his seat, pointed to the bar. "Do you see that man with the glasses and mustache standing by the far wall? That is Zephyr. He is from Haiti. He owns this place. The bartender? See her, the tall Korean woman? That is Janet. The man she is talking to,

with the shaved head and the suit? That is her husband,
Felix. He is from Haiti also."

Heller shook his head, trying to get the information
straight. "You said you'd been in New York for around a
year."

"Yes."

"You have a lot of friends."

"You must have several, then, if you have lived here all
your life."

"I know people." Heller shrugged. "On the job, I meet
people, in their apartments, their homes. . . . I know lots of
people."

"What about all those who applaud you in the streets?"

It dawned on Heller that Salim must have seen him before that day. "Well, that's different. . . . Those aren't really
friends, the people who've seen me on my bike."

"I have seen you on your bike. . . ."

Heller didn't say anything.

Wanda the waitress arrived with their drinks. She
handed Salim his gin and tonic, handed Heller his ginger
ale. Heller mumbled an embarrassed thank-you, waited for
her to leave before telling Salim, "My father doesn't mind if
I drink, you know."

"Your father is a long way from here."

Heller stared at Salim and drank his ginger ale.

"ADASI!"

Salim turned to the door, his eyes alight. "Velu!
Christoph!"

Heller's head shot up from his glass. Walking into Creole Nights was Christoph Toussaint. He was accompanied
by a wiry Indian man with the features of a clever fox

etched into the lines of his face. The two of them hugged Salim, and Christoph was about to introduce himself to Heller when he suddenly realized there was no need.

"Bike boy!" Christoph's grin widened. "Twice in two days, my friend!"

Heller was astonished. "Hello."

"You two know each other?" Salim asked.

"Saved my life, man," Christoph said.

"Well." Salim looked pleased. "It appears you do have friends, Heller."

"It appears I'm going to have to introduce myself," the Indian man said, extending his hand. "My name is Velu."

"Velu." Heller met his hand with a tight shake.

"Who wants drinks?" Christoph asked, turning to Heller. "What do you need, bike boy?"

"Jack Daniel's . . ."

"JACK DANIEL'S FOR THE MESSENGER!"

"No," Salim insisted. "He is fine. I am fine. Get Velu a Bombay gin and get yourself some of that French poison you like so much."

"Rémy Martin isn't poison," Christoph insisted, walking to the bar and greeting the rest of the regulars. Creole Nights was starting to fill up, energy building rapidly and crawling up the walls, filling the gaps between customers. Heller found himself looking in five directions at once, wishing for a second set of ears, eyes, a need to taste the air he was breathing.

"It appears I do need another drink, after all," Salim observed. He stood, offered his seat to Velu, then went to catch up with Christoph. Velu sat in one fluid motion, looked as though he could be comfortable in any situation. Adaptable.

"You are a messenger?" he asked Heller.

"Bike messenger, yeah."

"And that's how you know Salim?"

"And Christoph."

"It's a small world."

"This is a small bar."

"Exactly."

Heller caught himself having a conversation, struggled to forget it, tried to say something else and couldn't. He bit his lip and waited for Velu to say something.

"So you brought Salim some good news?"

"Salim seems to think so," Heller said hesitantly, pretending to be engrossed with the bubbles in his drink. "How do you know him?"

"He . . . works for me. I needed a good man who could sell books, had a good feel for them. He was a librarian back in Istanbul. He knows everything about books, speaks eight different languages."

"So you're his boss."

"I supply him with the books. . . ."

"Who do you work for?"

Velu took his time answering. He lit a bidi. The smoke carried with it the vague scent of talc, taking Heller back momentarily to when he was four years old.

"I went to India when I was four," he told Velu.

"By yourself?" Velu asked.

"Yes," Heller answered.

"Me too."

Salim and Christoph returned to the table, laughing loudly, sat down, and distributed the drinks.

"Are you all right, Heller?" Salim asked.

"Yeah."

"Velu is treating you well, I hope."

"I treat everyone well," Velu said.

"Well . . . ," Salim said, not bothering to finish his sentence.

"Well, well," Christoph amended.

Pause.

Everyone burst out laughing at once for no reason. Heller joined in, and the alarm in his face at hearing his own laugh wasn't missed by anyone. The laughter continued simply because it was there, and Salim raised his glass:

"To Paris!"

"Paris, France, or Paris, Texas?" Heller asked.

"Paris of Troy—who else would it be?" Velu said.

"The man who pulled it off!" Salim continued in a mad burst of words. "He came to her with nothing but a promise from the goddess of love and snatched Helen from under her husband's nose and all the rest of those Greeks!"

"I can see it's going to be one of those nights," Christoph sighed.

"The rest of those Greeks laid siege to Troy for ten years," Velu told Salim.

"We've had this conversation," Christoph said.

"The *rest of those Greeks* burned the city to the ground!" Velu continued, voice raised over the noise of the bar. "The *rest of those Greeks* raped and murdered everything in sight, and for those ten years, Paris didn't even have the courage to fight!"

"But . . ." Salim held up his hand. "For those ten years he made love to Helen every single morning, afternoon, and night."

Heller coughed, moved around in his seat.

"Salim claims his father was from what used to be Troy," Velu explained to Heller. "So Salim believes that gives him some sort of extrasensory insight. After all, who needs Homer, historical documentation, and the nine cities of Troy discovered over two hundred years by over two dozen archaeologists?"

Christoph nudged Heller. "It's interesting the first five hundred times you hear them arguing. The next thousand times, not so much."

"Then leave," Velu said.

"Yes, leave," Salim agreed.

"Ah, to hell with it." Christoph raised his glass. "To Paris and Nizima."

Everyone drank except Heller, who tried his best to appear invisible.

"So when is she getting here?" Velu asked. "When does the war begin? Because you know they'll be coming after her, and if the storm clouds are gathering, I stand to lose my best book vendor—"

"*You,*" Salim told him, "aren't going to lose anything. Nizima isn't coming."

The conversation was shot down in midstride. Velu and Christoph looked at Salim, who did nothing to further the topic, just stirred his drink rhythmically. The sounds of the bar magnified themselves, all coming to rest at their table: glasses clinking, chairs scraping against the floor, a burst of laughter from Zephyr and his staff. Detailed silence, thick with cigarette smoke.

Velu turned to Heller, looking for something.

Heller looked right back, then shook his head. "She's not coming."

Velu and Christoph exchanged glances, understanding how they all came to be there. Christoph nudged Heller for the second time that night, for the third time in two days:

"Tell him what you told me, bike boy."

Heller turned to Salim.

Salim looked calm. Sad and accepting. Nizima was a thousand miles away, and it was a hell of a distance to cram into a single moment.

Heller didn't speak.

"Sometimes it is all right to keep things to oneself," Salim told him. "Only sometimes, though. Sometimes it's all right."

The band began tuning their instruments, and the lights dimmed, shadows and light mixing by the glow of a dozen candles.

"To Paris and Nizima," Heller said.

They all toasted and downed the rest of their drinks.

The band was on its second break of the night.

Just about every seat in Creole Nights had been claimed, some more than once and by several different customers. The air underground had grown intense, a steady stream on the brink of rapids. The familiar eyes of a hundred strangers in off the streets, drawn by the sounds below. Drink by drink, the minutes passed, marked by the glow of an electric clock hung high over the end of the bar.

The glow of an electric clock that Heller hadn't looked at once since setting foot through the door. It must have been hours—he wasn't sure. His head swam effortlessly in his surroundings. Over the course of the evening he had slowly felt himself dissolving into his surroundings, a gradual sense that at some point it no longer mattered where Heller began and the bar ended.

Eternity.

Christoph and Velu had ventured to the other end of the bar earlier, and now Heller was listening to Salim and a twenty-two-year-old named Lucky Saurelius engage in some form of debate.

"And you think love is unimportant?" Salim accused.

"I said it was dangerous," Lucky clarified.

"Not worth the risk, eh?"

"I didn't say that."

"What are you saying?" Salim laughed, put an arm around Lucky with pure affection. "You writers are all the same! Nobody understands you until you put pen to paper!"

"Nobody understands us even after we put pen to paper, but by that point nobody wants to admit it."

Salim laughed, turned to Heller. "Love, my friend. What about it?"

"I don't know," Heller said. He glanced at Lucky, saw him watching closely, eyes accompanied by early signs of dark semicircles underneath. "Do you have a girlfriend, Lucky?"

Lucky lit a cigarette, took a drink of his beer. "I used to have a girlfriend. Her name is Helena. . . . She's in Paris now."

"Paris, France, or Paris, Texas?"

"Ah, Paris," Salim interjected wistfully.

"The first one," Lucky said. "Paris, France."

"Is she from Paris?"

"She's from New Jersey."

"Are you from New Jersey?"

"Lucky is from Chile," Salim said, then noticed something. "What's that?"

"What's what?" Heller asked.

Salim pointed to the drink in front of Heller.

Heller looked at Lucky.

Lucky looked at Salim, said, "Jack and Coke," and, before Salim could say anything, added, "I bought it for him."

"When?"

"When you were in the bathroom," Heller said.

"That was an hour and a half ago."

Lucky and Heller looked at each other, a pair of children caught with an armful of cookies before dinner.

"And then I bought him another one," Lucky admitted.

"And another one," Heller said.

"And then another one, I suppose?" Salim asked.

"Yes," the two of them confessed.

Salim nodded. "Well . . . we are in a bar." He put a hand on Heller's shoulder, squeezed. "And we are all friends, so if it has to happen anywhere, at least it is among those we care about."

Salim stood up and walked to the bar. Heller watched him leave, eyes full of wonder. Salim began talking to Zephyr, relaying a story, full of excitement and a charisma that demanded attention. Heller remembered something and turned back to Lucky.

"You were born in Chile?" Heller asked, interested.

"I was born in Amsterdam."

"Are you Dutch?"

"No."

"You're Chilean, though, right?"

"My parents are, I lived there for a while; doesn't make me Chilean."

"So . . ." Heller was trying to put it together. "You're American."

Lucky's eyes focused inward for a moment. He shrugged slightly. "I don't know what it means to be American. Do you know what it means?"

Heller shook his head.

"Hard to understand . . . ," Lucky said. "Just look at Salim. Half and half."

"Half and half of what?"

"Half and half of . . . everything." Lucky let smoke trickle from his lips. "Half spiritualist, half sensualist. Half Turk, half Kurd. Half sane, half madman. Half saint, half fool." Salim's voice burst through the din of the bar, a proclamation about Paris. "And by the end of tonight, I suspect, half gin, half tonic."

Heller nodded. He let his eyes wander, left Lucky to his own thoughts. He reached into his pocket and pulled out the picture he had taken from Silvia earlier that day. He held it close, squinted in the face of all that late-night light. Form slowly began to take shape as his eyes adjusted. Silvia sitting by a window, reading a book, unaware of the camera's presence, playing with a strand of hair. Dressed in an undershirt and orange shorts. Sunlight was pouring over her, giving her a yellow aura. She looked like a blissfully uniformed goddess.

Heller glanced up, saw Lucky lost, mind elsewhere. "Lucky?"

Lucky snapped to attention in one swift movement, waved for Heller to go on.

"Do you know anything about Chilean women?"

Lucky gave a slight smile. Very slight, as though his lips were remembering a fuller version that had been there at some point far past. He lit a cigarette and took a pull at his beer. "My first true love," he said. "My first true love, the one that still seems true in retrospect, she was Chilean."

"What was she like?"

Lucky thought about it before saying, "She understood the importance of staying up until dawn."

"So you know some things about Chilean women. . . ."

"If I did, I'd probably still be with her." Lucky glanced at the picture Heller was holding. He nodded, understanding. "You should speak to someone else about these things. You should speak to Salim. . . ."

Lucky stood, a sadness mixed among his cigarette smoke. He grabbed Wanda's arm as she walked by, drew her close.

"Dance with me, Wanda," he said.

"You miss Helena?"

Lucky nodded.

"Oh, Lucky, you poor lunatic."

"The world's coming to an end, Wanda."

"I know."

"Let's dance."

Wanda put her arms around Lucky and the two started swaying to the music. The Haitians at the end of the bar riled up in a chorus of yells and cheers of encouragement. Zephyr, Velu, and Christoph put their hands together, laughing.

"*Music!*" Zephyr yelled.

Heller watched them dance. His mind began to whirl lightly, the room losing its edge, falling into itself, a very subtle tilt. Heller watched Lucky and Wanda dance, eyes closed, floating with their feet ten steps under city streets.

"Jealous, my young friend?"

Heller found that Salim had managed to sneak back to the table. Leaning back in his chair, legs crossed, crafty expression full of mirth.

"Why would I be jealous?" Heller asked.

"Wanda is beautiful—you told me earlier."

Heller glanced down at the photograph in his hands, then handed it over to Salim. Salim accepted it, took his time looking over it. He glanced up, stared at Heller.

"I have a girlfriend," Heller said, tossing his shoulders back, sticking out his chest, and downing his drink. "I don't have to be jealous of anyone."

Salim continued to stare at him.

The song ended, and applause filled the room.

"You have a girlfriend," Salim said. "That deserves a drink."

"Allow me," Heller said, standing up.

He walked to the bar with a spring in his step. Cut through the crowd, managed to squeeze his way between two seats and motion for Janet, the bartender. "Gin and tonic, Jack and Coke!"

Janet nodded, went for the drinks, taking in three other orders and barking commands to the other staff on the floor.

Heller looked around, still wondering at the sudden change in dimension the bar had taken. He looked down the bar. Heller frowned, blinked, eyelids scraping against his eyeballs.

There, at the farthest end, sitting in a corner, was Dimitri Platonov. He was alone, brooding over a Stolichnaya on the rocks. Next to him, seated in place of company, was the rest of the bottle. Heller saw Dimitri finish his drink, take the bottle, and refill his glass.

It was like watching the sun come out in the middle of the night, a falling star moving up toward the sky. Heller began to walk over. Slowly. Cautiously, wondering what had brought Dimitri underground, if he was even there. Shoulders, elbows, and hips rubbed against him, words jumbled, dissected, re-forming in his head from a hundred different mouths.

He made it to the end of the bar.

"Gin and tonic, Jack and Coke, bike boy!"

Heller turned around, saw Janet slide the drinks in front of him, both adorned with red straws.

"How much?" he asked.

"Christoph's buying!"

Heller looked across the room, saw Christoph wave. He waved back, picked up his drinks, turned back to Dimitri.

Turned back to an empty table.

Heller looked around, caught sight of the door to the bar closing, someone hurrying up the stairs, out into the night. He jostled his way through the crowd again, drink in either hand, their contents sloshing around, small waves breaking free, running down his hands, dripping onto the floor.

He made it to the door. Looked through the glass, up the steps.

No sign of Dimitri.

It was deep nighttime.

Heller's bike was still chained to the tree, just as he had left it.

He stood there for a long time.

chapter fourteen

They emerged from Creole Nights, out into the open, laughing like a couple of fools.

Heller was drunk.

Salim was doing an admirable job of holding his liquor as well as holding Heller upright as they made their way over to Heller's bike. Salim's laughter died down and he began to sing, Turkish words, meaning lost to Heller.

"Ondort binyil gezdim pervanelikde . . ."

Heller dropped his chin onto his chest, tried singing along. "Ondo inle, guess dim, punderva . . ."

"No, no," Salim corrected. *"Ondort."*

"Ondor . . ."

". . . Binyil."

"Bindeal . . ."

"Pervanelikde . . ."

"Per—" Heller burped. "Pervanedlined."

It set them off laughing again. A couple walked by, saw the pair slapping each other on the back, and drew closer to each other. Salim tried to help Heller onto his bike while Heller looked after the frightened couple.

"My girlfriend is so beautiful," Heller said, words slurred.

"Hmm." Salim crossed his arms. "What is her favorite author?"

"She's got eyes . . . ," Heller continued. "Eyes, Salim, so dark you could just . . . fall into them. Lose your keys."

"How do you spend time together?"

"Fantastic body . . ."

"Heller?"

"Unbelievable smile . . ."

"What's her last name?"

Heller raised his head, steadied it. "What?"

"What's her last name?"

Heller thought about it. Thought about it some more.

"Heller?"

"Yes, sir!"

"You don't have a girlfriend."

Heller was about to protest, stopped. He nodded drunkenly, gave Salim a pat on the shoulder.

"To Paris."

He started pedaling down the sidewalk. It wouldn't keep still, and Heller wobbled, stopped, and toppled over into a pile of full garbage cans. He stared up at the sky through the branches of a tree, didn't see any stars. Water from that day's rainstorm dampened his shirt, soaked into his skin.

Salim entered his field of vision.

Heller smiled up at him.

"Heller," Salim said, arms still crossed, "you don't have a girlfriend."

"Yeah, well, you don't have a girlfriend, either."

Salim stared up at the skies, focused on something, said:

"What is she doing now?
Right now, this instant?
Is she in the house or outside?
Maybe she is petting a kitten on her lap.
Or maybe she's walking, about to take a step—
those beloved feet that take her straight to me
On my dark days.
And what is she thinking about—me?"

Heller sighed, made himself comfortable in the trash. "Nazim Hikmet?"

"You remember."

Heller smiled slightly, held up a small wooden horse.

"Look what I found. . . ."

Salim nodded.

Heller lost track of his senses. . . .

chapter fifteen

He remembered a few things.

Salim walking down a small city street, lit by the orange of streetlights. Heller hanging off him, trying to mumble words of caution, that his bike should be handled softly. Salim slowing his steps to make sure the bike didn't suffer too much damage. An intersection, Salim mentioning something about Nizima, something about standing free under the sky with no walls to imprison the sight of the night stars. Heller stopping at a bench, sitting down, throwing up. Salim offering a handkerchief. A stray dog sometime later. The door to his grandparents' apartment. Lying in bed, on his stomach, holding Silvia's photograph in his hand. Watching her closely.

Barely able to stay awake.

chapter sixteen

It didn't sound like his alarm clock.

Heller just assumed. He stirred, opened his eyes.

It was morning. The sunlight cut through his eyes, and he snapped them shut. He let out a meager whimper. His mouth was dry, the corners of his lips decorated with spit. Sweat covered his body. Heller had forgotten to get out of his clothes. The evening's events came back to him disguised as a headache. The sound of his alarm continued on through this, and it slowly dawned on Heller that it was the phone.

Phone call.

Slowly, very slowly, Heller rolled onto his back. He reached out, picked up the phone, trying to move as little as possible. Put the receiver to his ear.

"Hello?"

Into his ear came a monstrous yell, "WAKEUUUUP!"

Heller's brain split in two, right down the middle, it seemed.

He shot up, tried to shake the pain away, and fell onto the floor. Heller's head hit the ground, ear still to the phone. The scream at the other end died down, replaced by the voice of Rich Phillips, loud and confident.

Mostly loud.

"A man with such a shaky future at this company has no business being late for work, Heller!"

Heller stood up, his sudden elevation taking the room for a whirl. He clutched at his head, confused, and looked at the time.

9:45.

"How fast do you think you can ride?" Rich asked, a challenging note ringing through the wires.

"What?" Heller croaked.

"Because I'm already out the door, bike boy."

From somewhere in the background, Heller heard the sound of cheering, followed by Iggy's voice, relaxed and reassured.

"Heller, you alive there?"

Heller looked around, searching for his shoes. "I'm not sure. . . ."

"Well, never mind that. Rich is out the door with your first assignment, but I've laid down money that says you can beat him to the punch. You got a pen?"

"I don't have anything, Iggy."

"Then listen carefully: Rukes. A Mr. Durim Rukes. Thirteen twelve Greenwich Street."

"Near the West Side Highway?"

"Just about, yeah."

"That's on the other side of the planet!"

"Not for Rich Phillips."

Heller spied his shoes, dove to the ground. "What happened?"

"You sure you want this one?"

"What happened to Rukes!?"

"Wife and two kids," Iggy told Heller as he put on his shoes. "Trying to get out of Albania, crossing to Italy. Boat capsized, hundred and twenty dead. This might not be the last we hear of this today."

Heller finished tying his laces, stood up, ready. "Thirteen twelve Greenwich Street?"

"Go."

Heller ran out of the room, stopped at the front door.

He ran back into his room and snatched the picture of Silvia off his pillow.

Back into the living room. Heller saw an empty space by the door where his bike should have been. His heart leaped into his throat. He sized up the rest of the living room, ran into the kitchen, saw a note lying on the table. Heller ran over, picked it up, and read it: HAM IN FRIDGE.

Heller crumpled the note, shoved it into his pocket, burst into his grandparents' room. Nothing but the usual. Backing out, he turned, headed for the door to the apartment, opened it, ran down the steps, two at a time.

Out the front door and onto the streets.

His bike was waiting outside, fastened to a parking meter.

Heller felt tears of relief surface.

And before he could wonder how his bike had followed him home, he was on his knees, undoing the chain, muttering the address and details of his assignment, wondering just how fast he could make his bike go.

Surely faster than Rich Phillips.

chapter seventeen

Heller wished someone were recording the event—he was that certain that world records were being broken on every leg of the mad dash to Greenwich Street. He actually felt his body stretch as he approached what must have been the speed of light. Fifth Avenue, everything around him became a streaming tunnel. It was as though he were going through pedestrians instead of around them, diving into cars instead of having them swerve out of his path, feeling his wheels glide inches above the surface of the sidewalks and streets.

He had already made it halfway across town and was now headed south, picturing Rich Phillips in his head. What Heller hoped was that the construction that had been blocking the intersection at Bowery and Canal earlier that week was still as much a problem for traffic as it would be for Rich. If it didn't force him to actually maneuver through the crowded streets of Chinatown, then at the very least it would slow him down.

Heller pedaled even faster, the whirring sound of his wheels achieving a high-frequency whine, setting off dogs left and right, barking and giving chase, knocking over more garbage cans and tripping more people than Heller could ever have hoped to manage on his own.

The day was blazing, and Heller mainlined the pain in his muscles and head into his bike, sweating bullets of alcohol. His sights were focused through the red spiderwebs pulsing in his eyes, acutely aware of every last detail standing out in the rush of oncoming danger.

A gigantic truck stopped abruptly in the middle of the intersection of Fifth Avenue and Eighth, large body plastered with a TOYS "R" US sign.

There was no way to get around it, and Heller tucked his head down, tilting his bike at a slight angle and coasting directly underneath. His hair caressed its belly and Heller was suddenly past it, rocketing through Washington Square Park.

He parted the crowds with a loud yell: "TO THE GRAND TOUR!"

It was an epic sight to watch the throng divide, split in half. It was like having a crowd cheer him on at the final stages of a race.

But Heller knew the race was not quite over, and in front of him, alongside Washington Square South, a huge construction site had been erected overnight. The same sort of obstacle that Heller had counted on to slow Rich Phillips was now in his path, threatening to spoil his scheme.

Heller had only seconds to think, but it was all he needed.

Rich may have been deterred by the construction on the Lower East Side, but not Heller. These were Heller's streets, and he was not about to surrender them to a construction site just because someone somewhere had gotten the notion that progress would be a good idea.

Bearing down, Heller rode straight past the construction signs, into a thicket of potholes, planks, and heavy machinery. Nobody had time to stop him as he careened up a ramp at top speed, popping onto the second story of construction. He refused to stop, determined to make history in his own eyes if nobody else's.

He didn't stop even as he sailed over the edge.

Airborne.

Heller thought he might actually be flying. He didn't look down at the sidewalk, just straight ahead, cherishing every moment he could with the view from up there. Weightless. Still pedaling in midair, effortlessly, with no concrete to interfere with his movements. The wind carried him, and Heller truly believed he had finally found the one spot in all of Manhattan that was an even, perfect seventy-five degrees.

He didn't even worry about hitting the ground.

When it happened, he would deal with it.

Rich Phillips swung around the corner and almost ran straight into Heller.

Heller was standing alongside his bike in front of 1312 Greenwich Street.

Rich dragged his heel behind him, came to a stop.

Heller was calm and collected, looked at Rich offhandedly, as though it was some sort of coincidence they were both there. Heller didn't budge, and the two remained facing off, as though there were still a race to be won.

Rich wiped the sweat from his brow and looked around. "So you got here first," he said.

"That's right."

"Yeah, well . . ." Rich spat on the ground. "I'm calling this a tie."

"How do you figure?"

Rich pulled out an ambiguously light green card; 4 x 8.

"I figure I'm the one with the message, Heller."

"You're the one with the card," Heller corrected him. "Either one of us can deliver the message."

"And who's going to stop me from doing it, bike boy? You?"

"Rich . . ." Heller took a breath. "It's already been done."

Rich's face fell. "What?"

"I already talked to Durim Rukes," Heller said. "I went up to his place, I sat down, and we had ourselves a little chat. This is me getting on my bike and going back to Soft Tidings after a job well done. . . ."

Rich's disbelieving look wavered. "Nobody's that fast."

"I am."

"What if I go in there and check anyway?"

"Sure. If you want to embarrass the company by being the second person to inform Rukes that his wife and kids are dead. . . . I wouldn't mind Dimitri firing you instead of me."

With that, it was clear to both of them that Rich didn't have it in him to remain skeptical. With his head start, he should have been in and out of that door before Heller had even cleared Fifth Avenue.

Rich nodded and looked like he was about to say something else. He rolled backward a few feet, holding Heller's eyes with his own. Then he turned 180 degrees and disappeared around the corner.

Back the way he came.

Heller let the moment stretch out for a while longer.

It felt good. It felt satisfying.

And it only lasted until Heller got back off his bike and chained it to a tree in front of him. He walked up to building 1312 and searched the buzzers, looking for the right apartment number.

He found it, pressed down.

"Hello?" came the splintered voice through the intercom.

"Mr. Durim Rukes?" Heller asked.

"Yes, this is him."

"Soft Tidings . . ."

The intercom fell silent, and seconds later, Heller was buzzed in.

chapter eighteen

"Damn it," Heller whispered to himself.

He was standing outside Soft Tidings, leaning back against the building, baking in the heat, trying to pull himself together. His stomach was growling, matching the diesel trucks that went by in tone and volume. Heller's whole body was shaking. Dressed in the same clothes as the previous night, wrinkled and dirty, hair a mess.

It was Sunday. Almost 11:30. The sidewalks were letting their heat drift into the sky, white sunlight returning the favor for everyone walking underneath.

Durim Rukes had been a tough one.

Heller closed his eyes, tried to filter out the noise.

The sounds of tires coming to an abrupt halt, the indignant yells of a driver.

Heller opened his eyes and saw a young woman in a flowered dress. She was in the middle of the street, carrying a baby, trying to pick up a suitcase off the asphalt. In her other hand and under her arm were two more suitcases. Beige, tattered, and bulging at the sides.

A cab was halted in front of her, its horn blaring. The

cabbie was leaning out the window. He was beating the side of his car with his palm.

The woman got a handle on the dropped suitcase, made a few paces out of traffic, then dropped all three.

Heller watched, frozen, as she once again tried to collect her belongings.

He didn't move.

A club promoter for the Limelight walked past, handing out flyers. Approached a pair of clean-shaved teenagers, stopped them just a couple of feet away from the woman, whose baby was starting to cry:

"Saturday night there's a party, only fifty dollars with this flyer . . ."

The teens took the flyer, the promoter continued on his path.

The woman looked up from her struggle, looked at Heller.

In the distance, church bells started ringing.

"We're all asking for it," Heller said quietly. He opened the door to Soft Tidings and stepped into the shade.

Iggy was standing at the bottom of the steps:

"I figured Durim Rukes would be a difficult one."

"What are you doing down here?"

"I was coming to check on you."

Heller frowned. "How did you know I was outside?"

Iggy turned and walked up the steps.

Heller followed. "Sorry I was late, Iggy."

"Don't apologize to me. I don't pay your salary."

They walked into the offices. It was dead quiet. Only a few messengers and office assistants. Snail's pace, even for the approaching lunch hour. Heller was mostly ignored.

Garland Green shot him an ugly look from behind an *American Bride* magazine, which he was researching for possible clients. A select few bothered to say hello for the first time since Heller had started working there. He realized that he didn't know any of their names.

Iggy sat down at his desk. "Did you write out a receipt, get a signature from Rukes?"

Heller reached into his pocket and handed Iggy a slip of paper.

Iggy looked at it. ". . . This says 'Ham in fridge.' "

Heller stood to one side as Iggy called over a courier and handed him his charge for the day. Heller watched the messenger go, went back to staring at Iggy.

Iggy looked up from the computer screen with an innocent look.

"Yes, Heller?"

"Got any work for me?"

Iggy thought about it. "No."

"Have I been fired?"

"Once again, I don't pay your salary, so I can't very well fire you."

"So . . ."

"So we don't have any messages for you to deliver."

Heller blinked. "What do you mean, no messages?"

"I said, no messages for *you.*" Iggy picked up a few forms and went through them: "Anniversary, fifty years married. Birthday, little Jane is getting a pony. Birth, blond hair, blue eyes. Graduation, degree in poli science. Marriage, Travis and Kathy. Son paroled, ha— Do you want any of these?"

Heller didn't answer.

"You look terrible, Heller."

"No messages?"

"Terrible but older. At least a few years."

"Nobody else from that boat wreck?"

Iggy smirked. "Let's see if I can't make things better." He reached into his pocket, pulled out a wad of money, and offered it to Heller.

Heller took the money suspiciously.

"You earned me a hundred and fifty dollars this morning," Iggy said. "And you were the one doing all the work. Your cut is seventy-five."

Heller looked down at the money, not entirely believing it was there.

"You're the best, Heller. Though I suspect you won't be working here much longer."

"What?"

The intercom buzzed. Dimitri's voice cracked through the speaker:

"Heller, can I see you, please?"

Iggy looked up at Heller, raised his eyebrows.

Heller pocketed his money. "To the Grand Tour."

"To the Grand Tour," Iggy agreed.

Heller went to Dimitri's door, opened it.

"Heller?" Iggy called over his shoulder.

Heller turned.

"What the hell does that mean, anyway?"

A shrug of the shoulders and Heller was back in Dimitri's office for the second time since his sixteenth birthday.

chapter nineteen

The television was on mute. A documentary about Reagan and the Cold War.

Dimitri sat at his desk, wearing dark sunglasses.

Heller sat across from him, wishing he had a pair of his own. Dimitri was drinking a bottle of Sprite. He took quick sips, returning the cap to its resting place each time. After the fourth nip he slid the bottle over to rest in front of Heller, made a motion to suggest Heller should try some.

Heller unscrewed the cap, took a swig.

Gagged, tasting an acrid bitterness under it all.

He put the bottle down, slid it back over to Dimitri.

Dimitri took another sip, leaned back in his chair.

"Did you know that vodka is supposed to be tasteless?" he asked.

Heller shook his head, wiping his mouth.

"But it isn't," Dimitri continued. "It has a definite flavor. An elixir disguised as water."

"You and Iggy talk exactly alike sometimes."

"What did you say to him?"

Heller paused.

Dimitri's face was serious, inquisitive.

"What did I say to Iggy?" Heller asked.

"What did you say to Durim Rukes?" Dimitri leaned forward, arms on the desk. "He saved for years and years for his family to join him and now . . . What is it about you? What do you do in there?"

"I don't know what I do," Heller answered, uncomfortable.

"What could an American kid possibly say to ease their pain?"

Heller felt a twinge of impatience, didn't need this sort of thing on top of his headache and the moans from his stomach. "What's that supposed to mean?"

"Well, you *are* American."

"I don't know what it means to be American."

"And I don't know how you could possibly understand their pain."

"I think very few of the people I visit understand their pain. . . ." Heller spoke with a deliberate confidence. "I think very few people in general understand their pain."

"Then what do you say to make it better?"

"Do you understand *your* pain?" Heller continued.

"I only want to know what you say—"

"What do you need to hear from me to feel better?"

Dimitri stared at Heller incredulously. His fingers stiffened around the Sprite bottle, and the plastic made light crumpling sounds under the pressure.

Heller was surprised at himself. His heart was pounding in tandem with his head. He was having trouble keeping his breath regular, wondered where all that had come from.

The Reagan documentary continued playing on the television, images flickering in an electronic fireplace.

Dimitri's grip relaxed, and his face returned to its regular status as employer: "I would be very curious to come along on your next assignment."

"When was the last time you rode a bike?"

"Rollerblades, Heller." Dimitri's voice was past asking. "Don't tell me you have something better to spend those seventy-five dollars on."

"Well, I can guarantee you, it *won't* be an elixir disguised as water."

Dimitri drew in his breath. . . .

There was a knock on the door, a turn of the knob, and Iggy popped his head in. "Someone to see you, Heller."

"Police?" Dimitri asked. His tone was as hopeful as it was apprehensive.

"I don't think so."

Dimitri nodded, turned to Heller with a genuine scowl. "Close the door behind you."

Heller got up, turned, walked into the main offices.

Benjamin Ibo was standing there.

Heller stopped short, recognizing him, unsure how to place Benjamin outside of his apartment. He looked around. A few of the other employees had stopped to stare.

Benjamin was dressed in a black suit. White shirt, black tie, white socks, black shoes, old and dusty. His face was solemn, quiet features drawing more and more attention with each passing second of silence.

"I just got off the plane," Benjamin explained.

Not much Heller could say yet.

"I just got back from Nigeria. . . . The funeral was yesterday. . . ."

The entire office was watching.

"Or today," Benjamin continued. "I'm still not sure, what with the time switch. Perhaps the funeral is actually tomorrow and I will have another last chance to see my mother's face again."

Benjamin took a few steps forward, stood face to face with Heller.

"Last week, I wasn't able to thank you properly. . . ."

All those eyes. It was a first for Soft Tidings. Most of the messengers never delivered the sort of news Heller did, and none of the office hands had ever laid eyes on a single client. Heller could feel their wonder resting on his shoulders.

"I'm sorry . . . ," Heller stammered. "I . . . don't know—"

"It's all right," Benjamin assured, holding out a necklace. "I know you are the messenger, and I know she would have wanted you to have this. . . ."

At the end of the necklace was a black stone, carved into the shape of a palm nut.

Heller hesitated.

"It brings good luck," Benjamin told him.

"I don't need good luck."

"How many times a day do you tell yourself you need oxygen to live? It's easy to forget what's all around you, Eshu."

Heller reached out, stopped.

He took the necklace.

"Thank you," Heller said.

"Thank *you*," Benjamin insisted. "For everything."

"I really didn't say all that much," Heller mumbled.

"You said very little," Benjamin concurred. "That was enough, Eshu."

He gave a light bow and walked out.

Heller put the necklace on, felt its tug.

A phone rang somewhere in the office.

Slowly the office started up again.

"Hey, Heller," Iggy said. "Who's Eshu?"

"Huh?"

"That guy called you Eshu."

"I don't know what he was talking about."

"Huh," Iggy said. "Well, we still got no work for you. Go grab some lunch, do some goddamn thing before anything else happens around here, Heller—if that is your real name."

Heller reached into his pocket, pulled out his picture of Silvia reading her book. Looking at her more closely under the office lights, he noticed she was reading *Don Quixote*. An old copy, yellow edge to the pages.

He turned to Iggy. "Iggy, can you find me a book dealer named Velu?"

"It's possible," Iggy said, hitting a few keystrokes on his computer. "Who does he work for?"

"I don't know. . . . He supplies books for a street vendor named Salim Adasi."

"Street vendor?"

"Yeah."

"Well, I can't help you."

"Why?"

"Sounds like your 'book vendor' is an illegal immigrant,

my friend. And on the subject of illegal, your 'book dealer,' Velu, is probably a thief."

Heller wasn't buying it. "Thief?"

"Street vendors don't always get their own books. Sometimes they get them from a fence. These are guys who know people who work for major book distributors at the warehouse level. They also know the guys who do the ground-level paperwork, so they can skim a few books off the top, sell them on the streets, and make a bit of change."

Heller felt caught, bit his lip.

"Don't worry," Iggy said, smiling, going back to his work. "The last thing a guy like you needs to worry about is arrest by association. I can't believe that bike of yours hasn't already been impounded."

It didn't make Heller feel any better. "So how am I supposed to find this guy?"

"Salim or Velu?"

"Either," Heller said innocently.

"I don't know, Heller," Iggy answered with an exasperated sigh. "I'm busy. Go see your girlfriend or something. Just leave me alone."

"I need to find Salim first," Heller muttered.

"Then go find Salim," Iggy said absently, staring at his monitor. It was clear to Heller that Iggy was going to be of no further help. He looked back to Dimitri's office. The door was open a crack and closed abruptly. Not fast enough for Heller to miss his boss looking at him. Not fast enough for Heller to miss the look on Dimitri's face. The same face he'd seen in Creole Nights.

Yes—an elixir disguised as water.

chapter twenty

When Heller walked out of the Soft Tidings building, the woman with the three suitcases and baby was gone. Just a steady flow of traffic and a few Chinatown residents.

He wheeled his bike down the street slowly, looking around as though searching for something with great deliberation. The sun was high in the sky, saturating the city with light and leaving few places for shadows to breathe.

Heller squinted.

Sitting on a bench in Washington Square with a one-liter bottle of water.

The park was brimming. Heller looked across the way. Some players were kicking a soccer ball around. Blues man playing his guitar nearby, seated with strangers, all bobbing their heads to their own memories. The old folks in white slacks and gray caps playing boccie ball. Dogs chasing each other in circles, darting from place to place on instinct, owners' futile efforts to command some sort of obedience. Children splashing in the fountain. All around, sunbathers and the homeless lying down with closed eyes.

"Smoke, kid, smoke," came the swift words of a passing dealer.

Heller shook his head.

"All right, man," and the dealer kept on his way.

Nobody else spoke to Heller. Nobody recognized him off his bike.

Heller watched a pair of grown men dueling with long wooden swords. The two danced their way across the park, their eyes serious. The sound of wood smacking wood echoed off the distant buildings. One of them managed to score a hit. They stopped and bowed down, face to face.

Then kept right on going.

Heller pulled out the picture of Silvia again.

"Heller, you're alive. . . ."

Heller looked up and saw Lucky and Janet the bartender. Lucky was dressed in what appeared to be the same clothes he had been wearing last night. He looked a bit tired. Janet looked fresh and energetic, yelling at some kids across the way.

"Lucky." Heller smiled.

"Janet and I were just going to get a drink," Lucky said.

"Scotch and water and a Bloody Mary!" Janet sang, delivering a kung fu kick to an imaginary opponent.

"You want to come along?" Lucky asked.

The thought of more alcohol made Heller gag. "No. No, thank you, I'm . . ."

"You looking for Salim?"

Heller was impressed. Lucky must have guessed, as he went right ahead with: "I can just tell. Very good at knowing what people are about. It's a gift. Just about my only one."

"Have you ever been wrong?"

Lucky thought about it, took a flask out of his pocket, took a pull. He smacked his lips. "Yes. A few times, yeah . . . but I don't plan to make the same mistakes again, believe me."

"Can you plan that sort of thing?"

"Nope. All faith, trust."

Janet laughed. "You're so full of crap, Lucky! I'll see you at the bar."

She walked away, ponytailed hair waving goodbye to them both.

"Janet's really got my number," Lucky mused.

"I guess . . ." Heller put the picture of Silvia back in his pocket. "So . . . do you know where I can find Salim?"

"Nope. If I were you I'd ask Velu."

"Do you know where I can find Velu?"

"Nope. If I were you I'd ask them."

Lucky pointed out of the park, across the street. In front of the NYU library, a few book vendors were stationed at their tables, trying to capture the interest of the summer students.

"Would they know?" Heller asked.

"It's a start." Lucky shrugged and wandered off abruptly.

Heller opened his mouth to call out his farewell to Lucky's back. Instead, he wheeled his bike across the street and began asking questions.

He found Velu outside the Barnes and Noble on Astor Place. Velu was sitting by the loading truck, watching a fresh delivery of books arrive, talking to a B&N employee and one of the truck drivers.

Heller kept his distance, suspicious. He bought a hot dog from a nearby stand.

Velu and the other two looked at their watches, nodded to one another. With a subtle wave, Velu turned and walked up toward the 6 train station.

Heller caught up with him at the entrance, called out his name.

Velu turned, pleased. "Heller. You're alive."

Heller regarded him carefully. "That's what everyone's saying."

"How are you?"

"I was looking for Salim."

"Try Christopher Street, near the 1/9 train."

"All right, thanks." Heller realized he was still holding a hot dog. "You want this? I'm not hungry."

Velu took it with a smile.

A crowd of people filed out from the train station, almost knocking Heller over as he waited for the lights to change. He made his apologies, crossed the street.

Salim was sitting at his table of books, engrossed in *Murder on the Orient Express*. He looked completely unaffected by the previous night. It was good to see him.

"Have you figured out who did it?"

"I found something better." Salim looked up without a trace of surprise. "A wonderful expression: 'beat around the bush.' "

"Do you know what it means?"

"No."

Putting on a note of playful eloquence, Heller answered, "To postpone. To elude the conclusion by trying to stretch the present out as far as possible."

Salim grinned. "I like it."

"Do you understand it?"

"I do, but you don't."

"My head hurts."

Salim held up a finger. "I have something that might help."

He reached under his table. After searching through a few crates, Salim popped back up with a copy of *Don Quixote*. He offered it to Heller without a word. Heller took the book gingerly. He looked down at it, gave it a few light hefts, looked up.

"Salim . . . ? What, exactly, does Velu do?"

"Ah." Salim understood.

"Well, I mean . . . I guess you know what I mean."

"Heller, I could work for numerous places." Salim's words came out in a steady flow. "It would still be illegal either way, and I have no problem telling you why; but I think you already know my status in this country."

"I do."

"And if I did take money from a legitimate business-man, still, not a cent of that would go to the government, Social Security. I would still have no insurance. But who-ever I work for would know my secret. There are many like me all over the city working in kitchens, storerooms, even in the schools. And they take the money because it is all they will get, and because they have put their trust in their employer that they will not be reported. But say a worker asks for more pay or sees something he shouldn't—I have known many who trusted the wrong people and were forced back to where they came from."

"You can't go back to Turkey?"

"I don't choose to put my trust in anybody like that,"

Salim said, ignoring the question. "I have no problems with what I do. Last year over half a million copies of the Koran were sold in this country. I sold three. People are still reading. More importantly, others like me, with no money, are reading. . . . And I know my secret is safe with Velu."

"You trust him?" Heller asked quietly.

"Sometimes it is better to trust a thief than your best friend."

Heller coughed, bit his lip, embarrassed.

"You understand," Salim told him, pointing to the book. "Now open your book."

Heller opened the book, looked through it. The illustrations were stark and nightmarish, drawn from a world Heller found eerily familiar. Monsters, ogres, knights and battles, a never-ending fight. On the final page, Don Quixote lying in a bed, old and dying. His few friends and faithful servants gathered around, faces contorted in anguish, Sancho's tears spilling liberally down his face.

Black-and-white print.

"After so many illusions and wanderings, the madman dies in his bed," Salim said. "The price of sanity."

Heller felt his throat tighten, looked around, suddenly sure they were all seconds away from death. Nothing. Just the traffic and pedestrian activities of a Manhattan Sunday.

The feeling wouldn't leave.

"Heller?"

Heller closed the book with an abrupt snap. "Do you know who Eshu is, Salim?"

"Eshu?"

"Eshu . . . from Nigeria, I think."

"I do not."

"You don't know?"

Salim raised his hands defensively. "Do you expect me to know everything?"

"No, but I just thought—yes, you're supposed to know everything!"

"Sadly, today I can only offer Cervantes."

"Here's what, though." Heller played with the chain to his newly acquired necklace. "This is the third gift I've received today, and it just seems a bit—"

"Who said anything about a gift?" Salim interrupted, that sly look playing on his face. ". . . Seven dollars."

Heller smiled, feeling of dread held in check once again. "All right, but that's my final offer." He dug into his pocket, hands closing around his cut of Iggy's bet.

"Good afternoon," came a gruff voice behind him.

Bruno the Bruiser had pulled up in his car, parked it on the curb. He was wearing tinted glasses, NYPD issue. In one deft motion, he had his door open, stepped onto the sidewalk, sauntered over, a twenty-foot giant in blue.

Heller and Salim were frozen in the middle of their transaction.

Bruno stared at the two, eyes motionless under the sunglasses. Not a trace of sweat on his face. Air-conditioned vehicle, that was it. Immune to the heat of the city. It wasn't even clear if he was breathing under that badge.

Finally: "It's your lucky day, bike boy," Bruno told Heller, then pointed to Salim. "He a friend of yours?"

Heller glanced at Salim, mute.

Salim remained blank-faced. "A wall standing alone is useless."

"Well, with three more walls, you've got yourself a jail cell."

Salim's face turned hard. "Don't talk to me about jail."

"Then let's talk about books. You got a bill of lading for these?"

Heller watched the exchange, worried. Salim either didn't understand or was making believe he didn't.

Bruno wasn't having it. "Proof of commercial legitimacy. Do these books belong to you?"

"The universe is an infinite library."

"Do you know why people call me Bruno the Bruiser?"

Heller was growing nervous, tried to remain calm.

"That's not in my books," Salim answered carefully.

Bruno turned to Heller, who jumped slightly, hated himself for being afraid.

"Go on and tell him, bike boy," Bruno urged, eyes taunting.

"I've heard . . . people say that Bruno can . . . hurt someone . . ." Heller had to force the words. "Can hit them with his club so that no marks, scars, or . . . bruises are left behind. Nobody really knows how he does it or—"

"He uses a towel," Salim said. "He wraps the stick, fist, rock with a towel, a sheet, a rag—anything like that will do."

"I thought you said that wasn't in your books," Bruno said.

"Not in my books . . ."

Sensing a new presence, the three turned to find an older, white-haired policeman standing directly behind them. Warm face, round body, thick hands.

"There a problem, Bruno?"

"No problem, McCullough," Bruno assured him. "Just that this Paki thinks he's smart stuff."

"He's Turkish," Officer McCullough corrected him. "And he is smart stuff. Used to direct a whole library in Istanbul."

"Well, in *my* city, he needs a bill of lading."

"Bruno, there are murders bring committed in this town." Officer McCullough turned to Salim with a tongue-in-cheek aggressiveness. "You were planning on getting a bill of lading, right?"

"Of course," Salim said.

"And I was planning on buying a book," McCullough concluded. "So let's forget the whole thing, Bruno."

Bruno stood between the three of them, waiting for someone to say something else.

He turned to Salim, pointed a finger.

Salim gave no sign of intimidation.

Bruno walked back to his car, got in. He blasted his siren and peeled away into downtown traffic. Heller saw the red lights flashing, growing smaller in the distance, turning on some side street. Vanishing. He realized he was holding in his breath. Let it out. His hand was still in his pocket, wrapped around his money, palms sweating.

"Seven dollars, Heller," Salim reminded him.

"Right," Heller said, slowly pulling out his money.

Salim went right back into sales mode, turning to McCullough. "What can I do for you, Officer McCullough?"

"Do you have what I asked for last week?"

"*The Joy of Sex*, ultramodern edition?"

"No, no." McCullough looked sideways at Heller,

blushed. "The, ah, Spanish dictionary . . . ultramodern revised edition."

Heller watched them talk, counted out seven dollars from the seventy-five. He glanced at Salim discreetly, back down at the cash he held. Taking advantage of the distraction, Heller slipped the rest of the money between two books lying on the table, tossed the seven in plain view, and coughed. "I should be going, Salim."

"I will see you soon," Salim said.

Heller didn't move. Everybody waited, McCullough fidgeting impatiently.

"What's the first thing you said to Nizima when you met her?" Heller asked Salim.

"I don't remember."

"How is that possible?"

"It didn't really matter," Salim told him. "You've got Silvia's book—go."

Heller took a breath, jumped onto his bike, and blasted down the street toward SoHo.

"AND YOU WATCH YOURSELF!" he heard Officer McCullough yell after him.

It was all lost to Heller as he sped up, blending with the traffic and the rest of it all.

chapter twenty-one

Heller took his time chaining the bike to a public phone, trying to stall as much as possible. Postponing the moment, corraling his resolve. Beating around the bush.

The click of his lock, and Heller rose to his feet . . . slowly.

He exhaled, ran his hands through his hair, remembered to breathe in.

Heller tucked the copy of *Don Quixote* under his arm and marched into the coffee shop, ready for whatever lay ahead.

The door closed behind him with the familiar whoosh of the air-conditioning, sights and sensations of the indoors hitting him all at once. And all at once Heller saw that he wasn't ready for anything. Least of all for Rich Phillips.

Rich Phillips leaning over the counter. Holding Silvia's hand. Holding her hand and flirting with pure grace, that raised-eyebrow smile Heller could only imagine himself trying. Silvia was smiling. It was one of the few times he had ever seen it, a smile from Silvia. Eyes bashful rather than hurt. Shoulders loose. A clear interest in whatever story Rich was feeding her, his voice coated with the scent of espressos and cappuccinos.

Silvia's co-workers all stood at a distance, impressed and approving.

Heller felt his clothes gradually become too large for him.

Rich turned his head in Heller's direction and fixed his eyes on him.

He kept talking to Silvia, all the while staring at Heller, a look as unmistakable as witnessing the world's greatest chess player think: *checkmate.*

Silvia didn't notice that the universe was suddenly revolving around her. Before she could, Heller started to back away, that morning's battle with Rich Phillips playing out in reverse. Heller backed up, past the regulars, their novels and unfinished manuscripts, out the door.

Back into the oven.

Heller strode over to his bike, muscles taut. Sunk to the ground, hard concrete against his knees giving sharp warning of a bruise that would form later in the day. Hands shaking, he tried to free his bike. Struggled, his face contorted with rage and self-pity.

The lock came loose, the chain undone.

Heller leaned his head against the phone booth, paused, tried to steady himself.

He got to his feet, dug into his pocket, and found a quarter.

Put it in the phone, dialed a number.

Put the phone to his ear, hot, plastic, painful, and welcoming.

Iggy answered the phone.

"Hey, Iggy?" Heller's voice sounded a bit too anxious,

but he was past caring. "Yeah, it's me. Listen, you got anything over there? Can I get back to work?"

He listened intently. His breathing returned to normal as Iggy relayed the information. Heller nodded a few times, forgetting Iggy couldn't see him. "Eighty-eight West Thirty-fifth Street . . . Apartment eighteen G."

"You doing better?" Iggy's voice sounded close to concerned.

"Well, I am and I'm not," Heller said, and slammed the phone into its cradle.

Fifteen seconds later, Heller was doing much better.

chapter twenty-two

Sundown.

Heller sat on the steps of the gazebo, looking out past an expanse of lawn, over the waterfront, New Jersey on the other side. Behind him, the Battery Park City apartments rose above it all, some of the most sought-after real estate in Manhattan. Loafers on the grass lay about under the reddish curtain of the day, waiting for night to call them all home. Joggers, relaxed couples pushing strollers. Kids chasing shadows, parents in slacks and sneakers, the nearby commotion of a friendly basketball game.

All reflected in the Hudson River.

It was an uncharacteristic side of the city. Free of aggression and kaleidoscopic activity. Flowing, regular, back turned to the traffic of the West Side Highway. An otherworldly spell cast over everything, agreeable flowers and bushes adorning the outskirts of green.

Center stage for utopia.

It was Heller's retreat, where he usually went at the day's end. Sat and scratched only the surface of humanity.

Put the mind to rest along with the sun. Better than imagination.

A mosquito landed on his knee and Heller swiped at it, missing. He waited to see if it would return.

Iggy sat down next to him. "That sunset ain't a bad piece of art," he said.

Heller was caught off guard, and any response he could have made was left to speculation.

"I'm surprised I haven't seen you here before," Iggy commented. "I hear you come to this place a lot."

Heller found his tongue. "How did you know that?"

"Nothing special," Iggy said, lighting a cigarette. He looked far too content. "Part of the job."

"Yeah, you seem to know a lot."

"My father watches the news to keep track of events overseas and south of the border. Events that may eventually come back to Soft Tidings. I stay localized, that's what I do. Not everything makes the papers, Heller. Dimitri keeps his eyes on the world; I keep my ears to the ground."

"What do you mean, not everything makes the papers?"

Iggy didn't answer. He looked like he was about to but just smiled at Heller instead. Heller smiled back, even though he still had not gotten over the surprise of having his general manager sneak up on him. He continued to stare at him, wondered how Iggy always managed to just *appear.* Something in his manner, a controlled cool, something Heller liked.

"Do you know about your father and Dimitri?" Iggy asked.

"What about them?"

The New Jersey skyline across the water was slicing the sun in middescent.

"Why do you think you ended up at Soft Tidings?"

Heller sighed. "Yeah, I know how I got the job. My father and Dimitri go back. I get it."

"I don't mean *how* you got the job," Iggy said. "I asked, 'Why *do you think you ended up at Soft Tidings?*' "

Heller didn't know what Iggy was talking about.

Iggy put out his cigarette, lit another.

"Dimitri was exiled to Siberia after he was let out of prison. This was many years ago, back in the Soviet Union. I wasn't born yet; he didn't marry until he came to the States. Dimitri has never really told me more than a little about it. He's my own father and even I can't get very much out of him. But I don't need him to tell me, I can see it sometimes. I think you can, too. . . ."

Heller didn't indicate one way or the other.

Iggy regarded Heller closely, looking for an answer. When he didn't get it, he continued: "There was no way for Dimitri to know what was happening on the outside. No messages, letters, phone calls, nothing . . . An entire year of this—no letters, no phone calls. You know the only way to receive news in a place like that . . . ? Visitors. And in Dimitri's case, the visitor was your father. . . ."

Heller finally let the interest show on his face.

"That's right, Heller. I don't know how your father got there, how he found out the story, or who sent him. I only know that he must have taken an incredible risk to get the news to Dimitri. And I know the news was that Dimitri's mother had died—my grandmother was dead. I never met her."

Heller gazed out over the water.

"And one thing I know for certain, because Dimitri actually told me . . . It was your father who gave him the hope to make it through. Dimitri told me that if the news had come in any other way, from anyone else, it would have killed him. Do you see where I'm going with this, Heller?"

Heller had it figured out but didn't like where it left him. He stood, picked his bike up off the ground.

"Dimitri never forgot that, Heller." Iggy tugged at his cigarette. "And he found a way to turn pain into business, happiness into money. Started off online, then realized the importance of a face to go along with the message, especially in these times when nothing seems real. News with a personal touch, Heller—my father may have established Soft Tidings, but your father inspired it."

Heller suddenly felt as though he had been cheated into something. He refused to look at Iggy, at anybody else around them. Straight down to the ground, and when he did speak, it wasn't in the spirit of conversation. "The question you really meant to ask me is, *Why did* anybody *end up working at Soft Tidings?*"

"It all starts somewhere, Heller," Iggy told him, breathing smoke. "This morning, when you came back from delivering that message to Durim Rukes and I was standing at the bottom of the stairs, waiting for you . . ."

Heller wondered what would come next.

"I saw you standing outside from the office windows," Iggy said, putting out his cigarette. "No big mystery there, Heller. I'd look elsewhere for the unexplained. . . ."

Heller didn't stick around for any further words or reve-lations. He walked away, bike alongside, gliding smoothly over the neatly paved brick walkway. The sun had sunk past Manhattan eyes, leaving behind only an array of colors to prove it had ever been there in the first place.

chapter twenty-three

It was evening again, and Heller was tired, lost in his thoughts.

He felt defeated, and the prospect of home didn't seem very real to him.

It never did.

He trudged up the steps, felt he was working against a down escalator. Up past the third floor. Behind one of those doors he heard moaning and the rattle of dinner plates on a dining-room table. He shook his head, covered his ears, tried not to think of Silvia and Rich.

Once on the fourth floor, Heller took the last few steps to his grandparents' apartment and dug around for his keys. From inside, he heard voices, loud and boisterous.

He put his ear to the door, heard someone telling a story:

"This happened late at night to a friend of mine. . . ." The voice was muffled through the wood. "My friend was wandering the streets of the city where we had been born. A policeman stopped him. 'Why are you wandering the streets so late at night?' he asked."

Heller frowned, pressed closer.

"My friend's only response was, 'Sir, if I knew, I would have been home hours ago.' "

Heller turned the key and opened the door to a burst of laughter.

Salim was seated with Eric and Florence.

Not knowing what else to do, Heller just remained where he stood, neither one of his grandparents noticing him.

"Aha," Salim proclaimed, lifting himself out of his chair. "Here he is!"

Heller's grandparents turned to see him standing immobile in the doorway.

"Oh!" Florence exclaimed. "Heller, welcome home, darling."

"Mr. Adasi came to check on how you were doing," Eric added.

"How I'm doing?" Heller asked, bewildered.

"After last night," Eric clarified.

"Oh, those are the same clothes you had on yesterday," Florence fussed. "If Silvia ever saw you dressed like that—"

"Excuse me . . . ," Heller said through tight lips, fists bundled at his sides.

He turned without closing the door behind him and plodded down the stairs with obvious frustration. The space in his head was almost filled to capacity after the day he'd had, and the earlier headache now resurfaced with a low buzzing sound in his left ear.

Heller was undoing the chain to his bike when he heard the door to his apartment building open and footsteps approach.

"I think you've spent enough time with that bike to-day," Salim advised.

"Actually, no," Heller said, voice hoarse. "I think I've spent far too much time with *you* today."

He could feel Salim, could see him standing motionless. . . .

Heller stood and turned on him. "Why did you have to go and tell them about last night! I go through a lot to make sure they know as little about me as possible!" Heller paused, breathing hard. "I thought we were friends."

"If you don't want them to know about you, then don't put yourself in a position where a friend has to take you home and get you to bed. Of course they knew about last night—*they* let me into your house last night."

Heller instantly regretted opening his mouth. "You brought me home last night?"

"Do you think you flew?"

"I don't remember."

"Now you see why people drink to forget."

Heller swallowed, trying desperately to remember what happened after they had left the bar. "Yes, that part makes sense to me now."

"And if anybody here should be angry right now, it's me."

Salim pulled out a wad of money. Heller's money, the seventy-five Iggy had given him. Minus seven. He held it up for Heller to inspect.

Heller couldn't keep the guilt off his face, thought about lying, then gave up.

"Do you feel sorry for me?" Salim asked.

Heller thought about it, then nodded slowly, ashamed.

"Is it because of Nizima, Heller?"

"It's because of everything. . . ."

"Everything?" Salim asked in disbelief. "Everything can't be going that badly for me; I'm still here. . . . But pity doesn't help a situation like mine, and charity has no place in a friendship like ours."

Salim tossed Heller the roll of money.

Heller snatched it out of the air. He looked at it, not wanting to put it back into his pocket.

It was a cool evening. Close to crisp.

"If you were to buy us dinner," Salim suggested, "I wouldn't have a problem with that."

Heller sighed. "I'm sorry, Salim."

"Don't worry about it."

The pair began to walk down the street, side by side.

"Do you have any special place in mind?" Heller asked.

"I do now. . . ."

An ambulance rolled past, lights quiet. Resting.

chapter twenty-four

It was a small, lively, half-lit Turkish restaurant.

Salim and Heller sat at a secluded table, eating kebabs and falafel balls. A musician sat on a table substituting for a stage, strumming his guitar, singing words Heller couldn't understand. Almost everyone else in the place was singing along, familiar with the song, close to home. Heller didn't know how to behave, how to act; felt as though his skin were glowing, drawing attention to him.

Still, the food was perfect.

"Did you remember to lock your bike?" Salim asked through a mouthful of lamb.

"Yeah," Heller said, taking a bite of pita bread. "Well, I didn't manage to unlock it, so . . ."

They kept eating.

"So." Salim wiped his mouth with a napkin and served himself more falafel. "Where are you going, Heller?"

Heller swallowed his food. "I'm not going anywhere."

"Well, you are certainly getting there in a hurry."

Heller stared at Salim. "Do you find that nobody ever understands a word you're saying? Honestly?"

"Very few people understand me."

"Well—" Heller played with his dish. "I think you're the only person who understands me."

"I don't."

Heller's face dropped.

"Well, not always," Salim amended. "Were you born on that bike, Heller?"

"My girl's in love with another guy."

"My girl is *married* to another guy. She is probably dancing with him right now. . . ."

Heller put his silverware down.

Salim stared past him, watched the guitar player tune his instrument.

"Salim . . . ?" Heller ventured. "You really don't remember the first thing you said to Nizima? My father remembers the first thing he said to my mother, remembers how he felt and everything."

The musician began to play a song. Slow and melancholy, a progression far removed from Heller's world, and he could see the notes swirling around Salim, finding a home in his ears, resting on his clothes, seasoning his food, cooling his drink.

"*Ondort binyil gezdim pervanelikde,*" Salim recited in a low voice. "Do you remember that from last night?"

"Yes," Heller said truthfully, voice low, realizing something was about to happen.

"*I have professed love for fourteen thousand years*—that is what it means. That is what I felt when I first saw her. I thought of this song. . . . I thought my soul must have been waiting through all of time for her. . . ."

The music continued and Heller recognized the words now, recognized Salim somewhere in there.

"I had gone back there from Istanbul. Back to my mother's people, the only safe place for me. I had never gone there, but my mother always told me stories. In her language. In Kurdish. Only at home, though, because everywhere else it was forbidden. She couldn't even give me a Kurdish name. The other men I live with in the apartment can't know, but back then I *made* myself believe that part of me wasn't Kurdish.

"But when I saw Nizima, I finally knew who I was. I thought I knew who I was. She was fourteen and promised to another man. We kept our love quiet for years. She told me she would not marry him, though she knew what would happen to her, what can happen to a dishonored woman. And I thought that if her father found out, he might kill me.

"Still, Nizima's father was smarter than that. . . . He sent his sons to Istanbul to find out."

"To find out what?"

"After her brothers returned, Nizima came to me. It was a moonless night, and now I am sorry that I can hardly remember her face the last time we spoke. Because she told me that the police were coming. That I should go, that I should leave Turkey and go. That I should send money and that she would follow. And I wonder if she didn't say that to save me, so her father wouldn't have to kill me. . . ."

Salim sighed. His breath was caught by the melody, whirled in the air.

"Now, after having brought myself to this city through every trick possible, every day running the risk of being deported, after having sent her all my money, after all this . . ." Salim tapered off.

The music continued, the restaurant following suit, everyone involved in their meals and conversation.

Heller didn't know what to do with this sort of emotion. Didn't know how to deal with it outside of work; didn't know if he could go beyond the walls of the apartments that made up his day.

"You couldn't ask her to return the money?" Heller suggested tentatively.

Salim shook his head. "The money doesn't matter."

"Can't you go back?" Heller asked.

"No."

Heller chewed on their conversation.

A waiter happened by and Salim stopped him with a gesture, requested a glass of red.

"Another glass, Salim, are you sure?" the waiter asked.

"God will understand," Salim told him.

The waiter nodded, went on his way. The glass of wine was at the table seconds later, and Salim swirled it, pensive, sadness reflected in the lights of the restaurant.

"She's still thinking of you," Heller said.

"She's dancing with her husband," Salim said quietly.

Heller shook his head, convinced. "I think *he's* dancing with her."

Salim gave a single-syllable laugh, smiled. "You're a smart boy."

"Not really," Heller said, awkward, picking up his silverware and continuing to eat.

"You have insight," Salim insisted. "You have insight, and insight isn't a gift if nobody listens."

"You listen . . . ," Heller said.

"I understand you. . . ."

Heller bit his lip.

"And it isn't easy when the rest of the world doesn't, Heller. When their ears and eyes are sealed off to what's right in front of them, blinded by distraction."

"So what do I do?" Heller asked.

Salim took a drink of his wine, put his glass down. "If you wake up to find your house burning down, do you try to escape as fast as you can, rush out of the house in a frenzy? Or do you slowly make your way out, even through the flames?"

"I run out of the house."

"That's what you do. That's what everyone does when the world boils over. What should be done is simple; and that is to slowly walk through the fire. Take your time. Slow down, because the smoke will char your lungs, your skin will burn, and the flames will finally devour your house either way. . . . Slow down."

"Slow down," Heller repeated.

"Make her see you."

"What?"

"She hasn't *seen* you yet."

Their eyes locked somewhere in the middle of the table.

They ordered dessert and coffee before Heller asked for the check.

chapter twenty-five

They were sitting on Heller's roof, later, each one in his own rickety lawn chair, looking over the rest of the neighborhood. The sounds of the city tickled their ears. In the distance, the buildings of the financial district climbed upward to heaven, hiding the Statue of Liberty from view. Neither one had spoken for nearly an hour. Quiet and introspective, thoughts playing tag outside their heads.

Salim extended his arm, offered Heller a drink of wine from a bottle purchased earlier. Heller looked at the bottle, groaned, shook his head.

Salim laughed, took a pull.

They continued to sit in silence under a half-full moon.

chapter twenty-six

The sun was just rising.

Heller was still lying in the lawn chair, eyes closed, one minute away from waking up. All around him, birds hopped, cleaned their feathers, called to one another. Light crept up through pale mist, chalk blue sky and orange horizon. Sounds of the night shift heading home, crawling into unmade beds, setting their alarm clocks as their neighbors' went off.

Monday in Manhattan.

On some corner, several blocks away, an explosion tore through the air, someone's car backfiring.

The birds all scattered, a dark cloud for an instant, then dispersing.

Heller opened his eyes. He squinted into the morning air, rubbed his eyes. Looked to his left. Salim was gone. Empty bottle of wine next to his chair.

"Good morning," Heller murmured to himself.

He stretched.

* * *

The water cascaded over Heller.

Steam rose from his feet, formed drops of condensation on the shower tiles, curtain, walls, and ceiling of the bathroom. The drops made soothing sounds against Heller's skin, streams flowing out of his hair, down his face, cleansing him. The past two days of sweat and drink collected at his feet, swirled down the drain.

Heller relaxed, gave himself an extra ten minutes to remain in his liquid cocoon.

Thought about Salim.

Thought about Silvia.

His mind wandered from there, and soon ten minutes were over.

The mirror looked unfamiliar.

The reflection, Heller's face staring right back at him; it was as though the two of them hadn't seen each other in a long time. A distant reunion years later. Heller fixed his hair, tried combing it back, to the side, parting it in the middle.

Gave himself a mohawk.

Heller checked the calendar, if only to make sure that he hadn't overslept a couple of years over. It was still July 9, 2001.

Fresh clothes: socks, underwear, pants, and his SOFT TIDINGS shirt.

Glanced back into the mirror, still only a vague resemblance.

Heller raised his eyebrow, gave a psychotically wide smile.

"Who's the new kid?" he asked himself coquettishly.

Heller decided he had no problems with what he saw.

He winked.

A wave of embarrassment washed over him, and he checked to see if any of his posters had noticed. They stayed put, emotionless and impartial.

Heller went to have breakfast.

Cold cereal and milk.

Heller hadn't seen his grandparents since storming out the night before. They sat at the table, not saying anything. Waiting for Heller to cast the first stone.

Heller ate his cereal, looking into his bowl for something to say.

He finished his food as quickly as he could, put the dishes in the sink.

"Your parents are worried about you . . . ," Eric said.

Heller kept his back to them, ran some water. "Why?"

"Because," Florence said, "we're worried about you."

"Mr. Adasi seems very nice," Eric began. "He just seems to be . . . influencing you."

Heller turned off the water, turned to face them:

"Salim is my friend. . . . He's my best friend."

"How long have you known him?" Eric asked with disbelief. "Two days?"

"Has it really been that long?" Heller asked rhetorically, aware that a part of Salim was answering their questions.

"What about your other friends?" Florence asked.

"I don't have any other friends," Heller told them, picking his keys off the table. "No other friends. None. I don't have any friends. I am as unpopular as dysentery."

It felt good to say it.

It felt good to see the expression on their faces.

"I'm going to work, kids," Heller said. "I'll be back in time for dinner."

He walked out, tossing his keys to himself, whistling lightly.

That morning's mist was still shielding the city from the rays of the sun. It was warm, a perfect day at the beach. The serene temperature of a postcard. Slow and meandering winds; even the passing cars only managed to whisper their presence.

Heller unchained his bike.

He was about to get on when he stopped. Took his time glancing at his watch.

He looked back at his apartment building and then wandered down the street, wheeling the bike beside him.

The city strolled by, pleasant company for a Monday morning.

Heller walked over the cobblestones and broken concrete of Kenmare.

"Ondort binyil gezdim pervanelikde," he sang to himself, thinking of Salim's story, trying to see if he could remember someone else's past, imagine love in a distant country.

Heller walked through the door to 1251 and up the steps to work.

chapter twenty-seven

Absolute chaos.

The placid pace of Heller's walk was shattered in a single moment.

Pandemonium had engulfed Soft Tidings. A mad rush of activity. Phones were ringing off the hook, office staff running left and right, couriers running right and left, Iggy running the computers, and Dimitri running his mouth. It was overwhelming, a circus whose clowns had all committed suicide in midperformance.

Heller took small steps into the room, dazed.

Garland Green hobbled past him rapidly. His right ankle was wrapped in gauze.

"What's going on?" Heller asked.

"Statistical improbabilities," Garland answered.

"What's with your leg?"

"I hurt my wrist," Garland snapped sarcastically. "What do you think, stupid? I sprained my ankle. They got me working the phones."

"HELLER!" Dimitri yelled from somewhere in the mass of confusion.

"Can I get someone to tag line fourteen!?" Garland called out.

"I'll take it," Iggy told Garland, suddenly out of thin air and at their side. "Get ahold of Rich Phillips's cell phone, tell him his day off is taking the day off."

"Rich isn't going to be happy."

"Well, Richard can send himself a telegram with his condolences." Iggy grabbed Heller's arm and drew him into the battlefield. "Babies, everywhere."

Heller was bounced around, dragged by Iggy, wildly trying to keep his balance. "Iggy, what's going on?"

"Babies," Iggy said with venom in his usually calm voice. "Massive and massive amounts of babies. Marriages. Divorces. Anniversaries. Deaths. Birthdays. Heller, Soft Tidings has become the center of the universe."

Iggy squeezed into his desk, picked up the phone, striking a dangerously unbalanced tone of friendliness. "Yes, we're putting you through to the Missing You department, sorry for the delay, it'll just be a moment." He slammed down the receiver, attacked his keyboard, talking to Heller out of the side of his mouth. "And half of the bad news we've gotten is that half of our messengers can't make it today."

"Why not?"

"They've got mononucleosis," Iggy said, getting an error message on his monitor. He slammed his fist into the desk. "THE KISSING DISEASE! There's not a single woman on the entire courier staff! Have we just got a bunch of sissies on Rollerblades who've got nothing better to do than give each other MOUTH-TO-MOUTH INFECTIONS!?"

Dimitri strode over, his bulk causing riptides in the sea of panic.

"Heller, what the hell is that in your hair?"

Heller realized he was still wearing the mohawk he had given himself that morning. His quiet apology was lost in the noise as he straightened his hair.

"Have you got the computers back at the third terminal?" Dimitri asked Iggy.

"I've got Simon working on that."

"You call Rich Phillips?"

"We're working on it, DAD!"

Dimitri turned to Heller. "And you're still here because . . . ?"

"Heller, I got two messages." Iggy threw the cards and paperwork at Heller, who promptly dropped them on the floor. As he scrambled to pick them up, Iggy kept right on: "There's a death and an abortion. After those, I need you to get back here double time once I've managed to prioritize these messages."

"WE GOT RICH PHILLIPS ON TWO!" Garland screamed from across the room.

"Feed him the assignments over the phone—he can sign in here after he's taken care of those!" Dimitri screamed right back.

Iggy grabbed Heller's arm again, all tension concentrated in his clutch. "Heller, we don't have time for long visits today. I need you in and out of those apartments *fast*."

"Don't stop for flowers," Dimitri added.

Heller shook Iggy's hand off his arm, horrified. "You can't ask me to do that."

"We're telling you," Dimitri countered.

"I can't *do* that!"

"Heller!" Dimitri leaned close, nose to nose. "There are one hundred and forty-nine children born on this planet every minute and we are being told about EACH AND EVERY ONE OF THEM WITH EACH AND EVERY PASSING SECOND AND THERE JUST ISN'T TIME!"

"GO PUT THESE DEAD PEOPLE TO REST!" Iggy commanded.

"Go!"

"GO!"

Heller turned on his heels and, adrenaline rushing, ran like hell.

chapter twenty-eight

This wasn't how things were done.

Standing in a spacious hallway, face to face with a wiry Puerto Rican man named Hector Quiroga.

Handing him the card, no flower or extra condolences.

"Mr. Quiroga, your daughter decided to abort the baby."

Rage mixed with complete loss in Hector's eyes.

"Why would she have done that to us?" he asked.

Heller could feel the seconds disappear with each beat of his pulse.

Didn't answer him.

Heller ripped through the city like paper, face grim, crossroads and traffic lights mocking him.

In a cramped kitchen.

A Kenyan woman with closed eyes and shuddering breath, asking Heller if her father had suffered before his death.

"We . . . don't really know that."

Checking his watch, sick with the dishonor he was bringing on himself.

Back at Soft Tidings, Iggy handing him more slips of paper, further news of overseas woes.

". . . and at the bottom of the list comes this one: a missed birthday."

Rich Phillips walking past, calm stride untroubled. "Have you got the printout yet?"

"If we can just make it to one thirty, we should be fine!"

"Iggy, the printout?"

"HANG IN THERE, EVERYONE, AND NOBODY LOSES THEIR JOB!"

The city remembering it was summer, heat blasting through the air, up from the subways and sewers.

A Polish man in an East Ninety-fifth Street apartment, holding a little girl in his arms. "You really can't tell me anything else?" A hardened, desperate expression, hands patting the little girl's head. "There was nothing else? No sign of her return, no message from her or her mother?"

Heller stood stoically, trying to maintain the business end of things.

The muscles in his jaw clenched, teeth grinding.

Down Third, over to Second, in and out of traffic, in and out of apartments, wristband of his watch irritating the skin, buildings losing definition in the mad rush, tall concrete structures becoming rows and rows of tombstones.

An Indian couple seated on their couch.

Death of a relative in a riot.

Her head in his lap, crying, sobs coming out in muffled, choked installments.

Her husband's face blank, trying to comprehend, waiting for the news to plant itself in his chest, to grow into full realization.

Heller clearing his throat, voice reserved. "If you wouldn't mind signing this, sir."

So much compressed into one afternoon.

Message after message, sickness followed by death, followed by who knew what else?

An entire world caught in the deadly embrace of events.

Event building on further events, aided by the passing of seconds, between which there seemed to be no time for compassion.

Just business, as usual.

Heller cut a corner, grabbed on to a bus for further speed. He wasn't even thinking anymore, wasn't paying attention, lost in the mire, trying to keep track of the death toll as it climbed up the thermometer along with the rest of them.

He let go, let himself pedal to his next destination.

Heller passed Salim, stationed a few blocks south of Washington Square Park.

Salim waved, called to him.

Heller checked his watch, didn't even catch a glimpse of his best friend.

Made it to Soft Tidings, ready for more.

chapter twenty-nine

Things had calmed down.

Simmered into a steady boil, the regular demeanor of the Soft Tidings office.

"How'd you do, Heller?" Iggy asked, filling out a form for a couple of repairmen standing by the coffeepot.

"I got it done," Heller said, handing him his receipts.

"Good job."

"It wasn't right, Iggy, doing that to those people."

"It's how things are done, Heller."

"Wasn't right."

"Some days, that's how things are done . . . ," Iggy said.

He thumbed through the paperwork while Heller stood by, not saying a word.

Heller went to the bathroom, ran water over his face. The mirror was cracked down the middle and he couldn't get a good look at himself. Water drained through the pipes, a hollow washing sound.

Garland limped in, carrying a copy of *Modern Bride.* "Maybe I can finally get some reading done," he muttered, closing the stall door behind him.

Back in the office, Iggy was holding a slip of paper, his face in the shape of a question mark. "What about the missed birthday?"

"Missed birthday?"

"Greta Anderson—her 'little boy,' Ralph, won't be coming home for his fortieth birthday as promised."

Confused, Heller dug into his back pocket and pulled out an unfilled receipt. He groaned. "I don't do birthdays, Iggy."

"It's a missed birthday; not the wreck of the *Titanic*, I understand, but there should be something there for you to get out of it—you can take your time, you've done enough for one morning. Tell Mama Greta about Ralph and go grab a bite to eat."

Crackle of the speaker, Dimitri's voice: "Iggy! Where's Rich Phillips?"

Iggy pressed the button on the intercom. "Said he went to get himself some coffee."

Heller felt his stomach turn.

chapter thirty

It seemed to fit in rather well with the rest of his day.

Greta Anderson was a sixty-five-year-old British woman with a muddled accent and hair as white as her powdered face. She lived in Tribeca, a quiet section downtown that rarely caught wind of the rest of the city. Her apartment was extravagantly furnished, neat and spotless. Nothing looked worn or used. White couch in front of a glass table on a white rug.

She didn't seem very upset with the news of her boy.

Heller sat across from her in a large armchair, moody and reserved.

A gigantic strawberry cake rested between them, complacent and untouched on the glass table.

"Well, I can't be too upset, can I?" Greta said. She spoke in a sweeping manner that roamed the pastures of conversation the way a cow with no will to live might. "It's not like it's a tragedy, is it?"

"No . . ." Heller kept his sentences tight. "It really isn't."

"The boy's successful, and successful people are busy."

"Yes."

"I suppose that's the life of a senior VP. And now he's got that new account with Ultra-Tech Rollerblades."

Heller could have strangled her for that last piece of information but instead offered an insincere "Congratulations."

"Time is like the passing of—"

"Well, Mrs. Anderson," Heller cut her off impatiently. "I'm sure you want some time to think about this, perhaps send a prayer to Ralph."

"Oh, you've been so kind," Greta sighed, oblivious to Heller's attitude. "Would you like some cake?"

"I really can't stay. Really."

"No, I meant take the whole thing. I only bought it out of tradition. Ralph loves strawberry. Go on. Take it and share it with someone you love."

Someone you love, Heller thought, a sudden relief coating his insides along with images of Silvia.

Finally, some kind of sign.

Greta picked up the entire cake and giggled.

chapter thirty-one

Heller was standing outside of Buns 'n' Things, leaning against his bike. Poised and ready, the strawberry cake balanced on his handlebars.

When Silvia walked out, Heller was filled with resolve. Even the sight of her sandals, those elegant ankles, couldn't put him on tilt. He let her check the contents of her purse, took his time, waited for her to begin walking before drawing her attention with a well-placed:

"Hey . . ."

Silvia turned, hair whipping into her face before falling back to the top of her shoulders. She looked at him, expression blank.

"Hi."

Heller's nerves woke up, came back to life, and his composure weakened.

"Hey . . . ," he repeated, hoping for another shot at being suave.

Silvia's eyes narrowed. "Don't I know you?"

"Well . . . a bit, perhaps."

Silvia didn't exactly smile. There was something ambiguous in her eyes, though—a spark mixed in with the faint hint of recognition. Something warm. Something new.

"I got you a cake," Heller blurted out.

Silvia looked mildly amused. "I work in a bakery."

Heller looked at the awning of Buns 'n' Things.

She was right.

"I . . ." He tried to think fast. "I got this especially for you."

Silvia raised her eyebrows, tilted her head. She walked over, now with an actual smile on her face. Heller could hardly believe it. She walked right up to him, closer than he ever thought he would get to her. Right next to him, her arm brushing against his.

Gooseflesh in the middle of July, and Heller had to bite his lip to keep pleasant shudders from going down his spine.

Silvia looked down at the cake. She made some sort of sound, and Heller looked down as well, focusing on the frosting, noticing for the first time that it spelled out an actual phrase:

Happy birthday, Ralph! Mamma loves you!

Heller and Silvia looked up, stared at each other.

Heller's brain kicked him in the ass as he looked for something to say.

Silvia beat him to it.

"What's my name?" she asked him playfully.

A simple enough question, and Heller still couldn't find the voice needed to say it out loud in front of her.

"My name isn't Ralph," she said.

Heller looked back down at the cake, just in case he had

misjudged, misheard Silvia, misunderstood just how misguided his decision had been.

Happy birthday, Ralph! Mamma loves you!

It was still there.

Heller looked up, right into Silvia's face, his own glowing bright red, a heat that gave the sun a run for its money. Grabbing for straws, the moisture of humiliation clinging to the back of his neck, Heller said the first thing that came to his mind:

"Would you like to go for a ride? On my bike, with me?"

The instant the invitation was out there, Heller knew he had made another mistake.

Silvia's face darkened, the same cloud that had been following her since the first day Heller saw her in the window of the coffee shop. It was raining somewhere far away.

"I hate bikes," Silvia told him, her tone serious.

Heller was devastated.

"What?!" It came out with too much force, startled Silvia. Heller tried his best to recover from this tragic turn, managed to lower his voice. "Why?"

Silvia raised her left leg. She rested her foot on the seat of Heller's bike and slowly lifted her pant leg. Up past her shin, skin as tan as the rest of her body, or at least the parts that showed. Heller was confused and elated at the same time. She lifted her pant leg past her knee, let the cuff rest there.

On her knee was a scar. An old one, no doubt about it, but a deep one. A purple sort of color, an exposed vein cruising the surface of her skin.

"I got this when I was eight . . . ," Silvia told him. "I don't plan to get on a bike ever again."

Heller was speechless. He felt trapped by his own tactic, trapped between Silvia and his bike. He looked down at her scar, looked down with her, the both of them lost in silent contemplation.

Silvia looked up into Heller's eyes.

Heller's heart skipped a beat.

"It goes farther up," she said with a husky edge to her voice, eyes wide.

Heller let out the breath stuck in his chest.

Silvia put her foot back on the ground, and her pant leg fell back down around the ankle of its own accord.

She kept her eyes on Heller's, expectant, somehow.

A couple burst out of the coffee shop, laughing and stumbling over themselves, breaking the silence, and that was that.

Silvia gave a light wave, as though saying goodbye. "Try something different next time, bike boy."

She walked away, down the sidewalk, in the same direction as the time Heller followed her to the post office. She left him standing on his own, with his bike and a strawberry cake, baking on its own in the sunshine. The flies began to gather, and Heller had no choice but to get back to work.

chapter thirty-two

Heller strode through the offices of Soft Tidings, the cake of failure still in his hands, right up to Iggy's desk.

"Anything for me?" Heller asked, determined, angry.

"We got something coming in," Iggy said dismissively.

"Do you want some cake?"

Iggy glanced at the cake. "I hate strawberry."

Dimitri ambled over, considerably more under control than earlier.

"Dimitri"—Heller was desperate—"take this cake, I'm begging you."

"Cake?"

"It's strawberry," Iggy warned.

"Well, I hate strawberry," Dimitri said.

Heller was incensed. "What's wrong with strawberry?"

"Nobody likes strawberry," Iggy told him.

"Ralph does!"

Iggy read the frosting on the cake. "That's just because his mamma loves him."

"DOES ANYBODY WANT THIS CAKE?" Heller cried

out, needing very much to rid himself of any reminder of his encounter with Silvia.

"Nobody wants your stupid cake," Rich said from a nearby desk. He was filling out his forms on a clipboard, legs kicked up. He stared Heller down, annoyed. "You got that, Marie Antoinette?"

"You see?" Iggy said, glad to have proved his point. "Nobody likes strawberry."

"I love strawberry," Rich said, tossing the clipboard aside and crossing his arms with a satisfied look draped over his face. "It's just that I already had some sweets with my coffee. . . ."

Heller and Rich stared each other down.

"Rich . . ." Heller couldn't help it, felt it come out before he knew it was coming. "You're a dick."

Rich smiled. "Interesting choice of words, Casanova."

"All right, that's real nice, kids," Iggy said diplomatically. "Rich, go bother someone else, or whatever it is you do around here. . . . Heller?"

Heller wasn't done drilling into Rich with his eyes.

Rich didn't seem the least bit concerned.

"Heller!" Iggy slapped his ass and handed him a slip of paper and a green card. "You've got one Magaly DuBois, husband died in France, reasons unknown as of now—"

Heller snatched the information out of Iggy's hands, headed for the door, still holding the cake.

"You don't have an ASAP rush on that!" Iggy called after him, words bouncing off Heller's back. "Rest for a few minutes. Don't kill yourself over this, Heller!"

Heller's stride didn't slacken.

"There's someone I need to see first," he said through clenched teeth.

Heller kicked the door open, cake weighing on his arms.

He took to the streets on his bike, furious and looking for Salim.

chapter thirty-three

Humid and sticky, that was the atmosphere when Heller finally found him.

Salim was bartering with the Jamaican umbrella salesman, trading a copy of the *Tao Te Ching* for a pair of black umbrellas.

"Hey!" Heller called out.

Salim and the Jamaican turned in unison as Heller burned to a stop in front of them.

"I need to talk to you," Heller said.

"Too late!" the Jamaican said. "Just sold my last two! Ha, ha!"

He wandered off, leaving Heller disoriented and Salim staring down at the cake on Heller's handlebars.

"Who is Ralph?"

"You told me to slow down, to make her *see* me," Heller blurted out, angry. "That she hasn't seen me yet. Well, she just did and I think I may have been better off before."

Salim was trying to be diplomatic. "Did I promise you an outcome?"

"What?"

"Heller, you have to understand that when Hector was defending Troy, it wasn't a question of outcome. The gods had already foretold his death. All he knew was that he *had to fight*, regardless of victory or—"

"Salim," Heller interrupted, "shut up. Shut up, or tell me something I can *use*. I'm *sick* of vague, cryptic answers to questions I don't think even you understand."

"You know that even *you* don't understand your questions."

"I know that you're giving me advice about women and you couldn't even keep yours." Heller was venting, speaking faster than tact or consideration. "You left Nizima behind, trapped in a marriage you *knew* she couldn't get out of, and *I'm* supposed to fight? I'm supposed to butt heads with Rich Phillips? Oh, let me guess, you're about to bring up David and Goliath, aren't you?"

"All right . . ." Salim's voice wavered under his calm. "Now I definitely don't know what you're talking about."

"That's right, you don't," Heller told him, getting on his bike.

"Does blaming others for your misfortunes really help you rest that much better at night?"

Heller stopped, incensed. He opened his mouth and found himself choking on any possible defense he could come up with.

"Heller, you shouldn't—"

"I shouldn't waste time talking to someone like you," Heller spat.

Salim didn't respond, his eyes still in a fractured expression.

Hurt.

Heller felt a sudden regret caught in his throat, a poisonous taste in his mouth.

He shoved it aside, hit the pedals, and took off at full force, leaving Salim to stare after him, hands by his sides, each one holding a black umbrella.

Heller turned down the first street he could find, eyes wild and blazing. He was trying all he could to bring himself back to his work, trying to remember where his next message was to be delivered, could only think of the name: Magaly DuBois.

He cut through Washington Square, right down the middle. A few scattered cries and salutations from the park life, but Heller ignored them, shoved them into some peripheral section of his mind. Let them all slide by.

Cut through an a cappella group singing a George Michael song. Baritones and altos turned to soprano screams as they dove out of Heller's path. Reproach from some, approval from a group of skateboarders nearby, though Heller didn't take note of praise or anger.

He sped past a flower bed, reached down low, and expertly uprooted a yellow flower with his hand. He held on to it as he exited the park, still balancing the malignant cake.

Turned once, twice, westbound.

There on the curb, ten seconds away, was Bruno's police car, parked with the motor on. Bruno was leaning against his car, making time with a woman with coffee-colored skin whose hair reached all the way down to the top of her knee-high, black leather boots.

She was smiling.

Smiling at Bruno's lines, broad shoulders, and superior build.

The sight made Heller sick.

He breezed past.

Slowed after a few yards, stopped.

He turned and watched Bruno in action, all charm, shiny badge, and well-fitting uniform.

A light drizzle sprinkled on the city, nearly invisible.

It was too much to bear.

Sticking the flower between his teeth, Heller rode back toward Bruno, a steady growl growing somewhere at the base of his stomach. He hefted Ralph's cake, Ralph's strawberry cake, onto one hand. Prepared himself for a moment of pure satisfaction.

"MAMMA LOVES YOU!" Heller screamed at the top of his lungs, voice grabbing the attention of everyone on the street, shoppers looking out of windows in surprise.

The cake flew through the air, a perfect arc, a rainbow of pure red.

It dropped, plastering the windshield of Bruno's car.

Flecks of frosting sprayed onto Bruno's uniform, drops of strawberry blood on him and the breasts of his woman.

Heller glanced back.

Saw Bruno jumping into his car, closing the door, and taking off in hot pursuit.

Kicking his speed up, Heller sped back to the park. His mind was racing, free of any thought, completely trapped, locked into motion and a never-ending moment.

From behind, he heard Bruno turn on the siren.

Its wail was almost immediately behind Heller, who had to respect that he could not outrace a car. Just as he felt the grille kissing his heels, the hot breath of the engine melting the rubber of his wheels, he stuck out his arm.

Fingers and palm wrapped around a lamppost. Holding on tight, his momentum swung him ninety degrees, out of Bruno's path. The police car blasted past him, a definite stirring of the air touching the back of his neck.

Heller realized Bruno might actually be trying to kill him.

He broke out into a sweat, heard Bruno doubling back.

The rain started to come down harder.

He crossed corners, almost colliding with an ice-cream truck. He sought refuge in the park, once again among the squirrels and summertime outcasts. The green foliage shone with water drops, beads of light streaking past.

Another burst of thunder split the sky, and Heller hit his brakes.

Before him was a policeman on a black horse.

The ground was slick with rain, and Heller's bike skidded of its own accord, stopping inches before the steed's hooves.

Eyes wide, Heller craned his neck as the black horse reared on its hind legs, pawed at the sky, towering over the boy and his bike. Nostrils flaring, spit flying through powerful teeth, and muscles tight like the thickest rope. Eyes cavernous and gleaming.

Heller reared his bike, mouth open in a silent scream, put his front wheel down to the ground, and peeled out, the dark horse following him, and he was certain there would be no escape.

All through the park, people ran in every direction, fleeing the summer storm. The rain was coming in sheets, turning the ground into a river. Heller wove in and out of inlets and the rush for cover, hooves crashing down behind him, gaining far too fast.

Against his better judgment, Heller looked over his shoulder. . . .

No horse.

Before Heller could reason with his newfound safety, he was out the south side of the park, and Bruno's car squealed around a corner, joined by another, pursuing him, their tires making waves.

Heller stood, lifted himself off the seat, pumped at the bike with every ounce of energy, his clothes weighing him down, lungs burning, breath coaxing the flames to rise higher through his chest. He turned left, hoping to catch a one-way street the police couldn't follow.

No good.

Immersed in his plight, Heller didn't notice when he blew past Salim's stand for the third time that day. Didn't notice Salim calling out his name, still holding one of the umbrellas in his hand as he waved frantically. Didn't notice a roadblock for road construction until seconds before collision. Eyes suddenly focusing on orange-and-black warning signs, brakes applied.

Too much speed.

Heller's bike tipped in midskid, sending him to the ground and crashing against a wooden barrier. Heller's legs were tangled in his bike, wheels still spinning, going nowhere. He stood, checked himself for injuries, could only locate a few bruises on his legs, shoulders, forehead. A bit of blood on his lower lip, quickly diluting with the water pouring down his face.

In an instant, he was trapped. The two police cars halted in front of him, Bruno's still caked with frosting, now a mush of crumbs and sugary residue.

Four policemen stepped out, Bruno taking the lead, drawing out his nightstick.

Heller felt a rush through his body, head elevated, rising far above all the conflict, watching from above, putting everything into third person, filling Heller with a frightened sense of defiance.

"You're coming with me, bike boy!" Bruno yelled, advancing slowly.

"I'm not going anywhere!" Heller replied over the roar of the weather.

"You see this badge?"

"Yeah, but it's hard to see you hiding behind it!"

"All right." Bruno was almost upon Heller. The rest of the officers were looking nervous, worried and ready, arms poised for action at a moment's notice. From behind them all, Salim was running to the scene, umbrella unconsciously brandished, trying to stop things before they went any further.

"No more cycling for you, bike boy," Bruno declared, only feet away from Heller.

Salim broke through the line of policemen, provoking a reflexive yell:

"Bruno, watch out!"

Everything after that happened almost too fast to remember later.

Bruno turned just as Salim was reaching out to put a hand on his shoulder. The policeman lashed out, dug his club into Salim's gut.

Salim doubled over. One arm covering his stomach, the other one held up, silently asking Bruno to back off, hold on a moment.

Bruno took it as a threat, struck Salim across the back.

Salim hit the pavement.

The other policemen stood by and watched as Bruno's blows rained down on Salim.

Head, back, shoulders, arms.

Heller watched in horror, paralyzed. Water gushed into his eyes, dripped off his face, blurred his vision, leaving him with only the wet, smacking sounds of Bruno's club to drown out every last detail.

Nothing but the sound of flesh tearing, the cracking of bones.

He blinked, and in the seconds before it was over, his vision cleared.

Salim looking up at him, those eyes looking into his eyes, that face a grimace of pain.

That face a trail of blood.

The rest of the policemen ran over to Salim, dragged him by his arms to Bruno's car.

Threw him inside.

Slammed the door with the accompanying clap of thunder.

Heller's paralysis broke, a sudden overdose of sensation.

The police cars had already begun to drive away, and Heller screamed for them to stop. Leaping onto his bike, he chased after them. Managed to take two sharp turns, his efforts valiant, but technology finally triumphed.

Heller's pedaling slowed, tapering off into a dead stop.

He watched the cars disappear into the distance.

The vanishing point spread out far in front of Heller. His breath came out in heavy bursts, mind running in twelve different directions at once, wondering where they were taking Salim, what they would do to him once hidden from the eyes of the city, if he would ever see his friend again.

The rain suddenly stopped.

All at once.

The empty streets were quiet, remembering the storm, keeping it close.

Then the slow appearance of people. Coming out from doorways and overhangs, searching through remains of the deluge, eyes unfocused, as though seeing things for the first time.

Activity again, the city restored.

Heller looked down at his hand.

Saw the flower for Magaly DuBois resting there.

Not knowing what else to do, shocked beyond the capacity to do anything other than what he had set out to do at the start of his day, what he was supposed to do, what everyone expected.

There wasn't anything else to do anyway.

chapter thirty-four

It was strange to be back to work.

Standing in front of another door, waiting for the inevitable answer.

It was as though nothing had happened.

Heller was amazed at the odd state of calm surrounding him.

He felt himself start to cry.

Stopped, bit his lip . . .

Suddenly all right, once again at peace.

The door opened.

"Madame Magaly—" Heller began, before cutting himself off.

Magaly DuBois was standing in the doorway, fresh out of the shower.

Towel wrapped around her head. Towel wrapped around her body.

She was maybe twenty-nine. Thin, angular features, oddly framed by full lips and eyes that resembled the indifferent flash of a camera. Shapely legs, excessive hips for a woman so thin. The leftovers from her shower still glistened on her arms, neck, face moist and shimmering. She stood poised, erect, clearly in her element.

She moved her eyes up and down Heller's body, taking him in.

Heller tried not to do the same.

"Magaly DuBois?" he asked, finally finding his voice.

"Yes . . ." An unmistakable French accent colored her words. "Who are you?"

"I'm . . . with Soft Tidings. . . . I have a message for you."

Magaly's eyes softened, though not with concern of any kind. If anything, they developed a certain light or sultriness to them.

She smiled. "Please, *soyez le bienvenu*."

Heller stepped over the threshold, making sure not to brush against any part of her.

She closed the door and led him into the living room.

All of the furniture was covered in white sheets. The entire room seemed to be filled with irregularly shaped ghosts, resting, too tired to shock or frighten. The gray light filtering through the windows cast a blue hue over everything.

Heller and Magaly stood face to face.

"Madame DuBois—" Heller began.

"Forgive me for making you wait," she said. "I was in the shower."

"Madame DuBois," Heller continued, determined to make at least one assignment work that day. "There's no easy way to tell you this, but I'm afraid your husband has died."

Magaly's expression didn't change. She just stared at Heller for a long time.

Finally, she let a very strange smile play around the corners of her mouth.

"You're wet," she said.

Heller looked down at his clothes, saw that he was still drenched from the downfall. He shifted in his shoes, heard overt squishing noises.

"I'm sorry," he apologized. "It was raining earlier and—"

Magaly took off her towel.

Heller froze.

She offered him the towel.

His eyes went down to her breasts, farther down, sure that his expression was nothing less than juvenile. His stomach stirred, an excited ache, a timid arousal growing obvious to both him and Magaly.

Magaly didn't seem to mind.

"How did that happen?" she asked, smiling. "The death, I mean."

Heller took the towel, didn't do anything with it.

Magaly walked into another room, and his hypnotic state momentarily dissolved.

"Nobody knows," he called after her, adjusting his pants. "Not yet at least . . . died in his sleep."

Magaly walked back into the room in a white, near-transparent robe. A misguided attempt at modesty, her body still openly displayed under the material. She walked past Heller, and his eyes, his entire head followed her as she walked into the kitchen and out of sight.

"Died in his sleep?" Her voice floated through the apartment.

"Madame DuBois," Heller began, flustered, attempting to regain composure. He walked toward the kitchen door as he spoke. "I know this isn't the way you wanted to find out. Believe me . . . I do this a lot. It's my job. But I have enough"—hesitated—"experience. Despite my age . . . to know that it is possible to move on, and that come tomorrow—"

Heller had made it to the entrance of the kitchen, put his head around the corner when he was greeted by a deafening POP!

A champagne cork ricocheted off the wall, inches from Heller's head.

He jumped, turned.

Magaly was next to the icebox, holding a bottle of champagne and two glasses. The bottle was oozing foam, dripping down the neck and onto the floor.

Magaly was definitely smiling.

"You can call me Magaly," she said.

"I would rather call you Madame DuBois," Heller said, not convincing in the least.

"Is it best to keep things formal in your experience?"

"Yes . . ."

"Then just how much can you have actually experienced?"

Heller had no answer to that question, and Magaly went right ahead: "I would very much like it if you would be the first to celebrate with me."

She walked past Heller into the living room, and this time she did brush against him, her right breast against his arm. She sat down, crossed her legs.

Heller remained at the door, veins engorged with blood, his thoughts nothing but a red strip across his vision.

"When I saw you standing at the door, I had this sudden

feeling," Magaly told him. "I don't know how to explain it. A sudden rush, I suppose. A feeling of comfort, familiarity."

"Déjà vu?" Heller offered.

"No. It wasn't déjà vu."

"How do you know?"

"Because—" She poured the champagne into the glasses, let the head rise to the top. "There's no explanation for déjà vu. . . . But I just knew that you were the one. That the messenger had arrived with the news . . . finally."

Magaly extended one of the glasses to Heller. He moved forward, slowly, accepted her drink, let her clink her glass against his, drank with her. Cautiously, as though suspecting arsenic in place of bubbly.

It irritated his throat and he grimaced. "Finally?"

Magaly took the towel from her head. Platinum blond hair fell over her shoulders, strands sticking together. She began to dry her hair, casual as she spoke.

"I hated my husband. I married him because I thought I loved him, or that he loved me, or some childish fantasy. I was young, realized very early that I had made a mistake, but he wouldn't give me a divorce, wouldn't give me any freedom. . . ." She picked up her glass, took a sip, bore right into Heller with her eyes. "Wouldn't give me anything . . ."

Heller knew this couldn't be happening, felt reality slipping away with every minute he spent in Magaly's presence. Her see-through robe, crossed legs, confident poise at the news of her husband's death, and what was there left to comfort?

"Look at you," Magaly said playfully, rising to her feet, robe partially opened. "Follow me."

She led Heller into a bedroom. At least, that was what it

appeared to be. White sheets covering everything, just as in the living room, and he realized for the first time that there were no decorations; not in the living room, in that bedroom, nowhere.

A mattress on the floor, light blue; no sheets, the only thing uncovered and vulnerable to the afternoon light.

Magaly faced Heller, little air between the two.

Little air in that apartment, and Heller slowly felt suffocated by it all.

"Lift your arms," Magaly said.

Heller felt small and ashamed, unsure where his feelings were stemming from.

"Lift . . . ," Magaly insisted.

Heller lifted his arms.

Magaly reached down, peeled off his shirt. It came off with some difficulty, stuck around his head. She tugged at it, managed to free it from his body. She looked at Heller's hair, all a mess. "You would look good with a mohawk," she said, giving a small laugh.

Heller lowered his arms.

Magaly reached for the doorknob and picked up a white button-down shirt that was hanging there. She threw it around Heller in a half embrace, slipped his arms into it, adjusting his body to better fit. Starting at the neck, she began buttoning; first, second, third, making her way down his body.

Her eyes cleaved into him, and Heller felt like a caged animal.

"I hated my husband," she said.

She moved forward, planted a kiss on his lips.

The contact sent electricity through Heller's body, and

he felt as though he might collapse, knees unable to sustain the events of the day, a sudden urge swelling, filling him completely.

Magaly stared at him, eyes so close they appeared as one.

"Death is a wonderful thing," she whispered. "And you are a wonderful messenger. . . ."

She put her hand to the back of Heller's neck, drew him close. Pressed her lips against his, and Heller was lost in her, the cut on his lower lip screaming in pain, asking for more, her tongue in his mouth when he thought:

She's been waiting for this news for fourteen thousand years. . . .

His eyes snapped open.

He pushed her away, more strongly than he had intended, and she ended up on the floor, seated on the mattress. Her robe was open, revealing, and Heller was brought back to everything, an immediate return to the present.

He took to his heels, ran out the door.

Magaly was left in the bedroom, her receipt unsigned.

chapter thirty-five

Heller leaned against a lamppost outside of Magaly's apartment and vomited.

Coughed, retched, spat.

Stayed bent over, shaking. Muscles convulsing, spasms racking his body.

Heller looked down into his hand and saw the flower, still there.

He closed his eyes, threw it into the gutter.

"Heller!"

Heller lifted his head slightly. He saw Benjamin Ibo approaching, body appearing slanted from Heller's off-balance angle.

He wiped his mouth, tried to straighten himself up.

"Heller." Benjamin put an arm around his shoulder, warmed with the sound of his voice. "What's up, man? You all right?"

"Benjamin," Heller croaked, coughed, spat, "I think you may have given your good-luck charm to the wrong person."

"What's the matter?"

Heller saw the concern in his eyes and thought he

might cry right there under the skies and scrutiny of the West Village.

Instead, he told Benjamin about his day.

Minutes later found them at a pay phone.

Benjamin was dialing a number from the phone book, Heller standing close by, supporting himself against his bicycle.

"I have a friend who works for the Immigration Rights Watch," Benjamin was saying. "He's told me about things like this. It is often procedure for cops to dump their victims at a hospital instead of having to fill out a full report at the station. If your friend is an illegal, then we should try the clinics before we go to the police to lodge a complaint. . . ."

Benjamin held up his hand, indicating a voice at the other end. "Yes, hello? I was wondering if you had a recent check-in of one Mr.—"

"Salim Adasi," Heller told him.

"Salim Adasi?" Benjamin finished. "Yes, I'll wait."

And so they waited. The classical music was overwhelming through the earpiece, so loud even Heller could catch every note.

"Benjamin?" Heller was amazed at his own voice. Tried to make it deeper, more forceful. "Who is Eshu?"

"What's that, mate?"

"Last time we talked, you called me Eshu. . . . Who is Eshu?"

Benjamin held up his hand again, spoke into the phone. "Yes, hello? Yes . . . is he all right? . . . All right, thank you. Goodbye." He hung up. "He's at St. John's. . . . They brought him in an hour ago." He smiled slightly. "See, first try. That good-luck charm is up to something."

"Is he all right?" Heller asked, scared of any answer.

"He's breathing. It's a start. . . ." Benjamin sighed, straightened himself. "My prayers are with you, Eshu."

"I still don't know who that is," Heller said weakly.

"My people's Guardian of the Crossroads," Benjamin said, filled with a sudden seriousness that outweighed anything Heller had previously seen in him. "More importantly, our messenger between heaven and earth. His job is to stir things up, keep the world moving through his tricks. But above all else, he is Destiny's best friend."

The weight of his words threatened to drive Heller into the ground.

". . . And Eshu must always be careful of his own cunning," Benjamin added.

"Thank you for finding Salim."

Benjamin reached into his shirt pocket, pulled out his card.

"I doubt this will be the last time. . . . Here's my number."

Heller took the card.

"I'll hear from you soon . . . ," Benjamin concluded, but not before adding his final words, the soft-spoken command that Heller found all too familiar:

"Go."

chapter thirty-six

The smell of sanitation wasn't resting well with Heller.

Between the white-colored walls of the hospital corridors and the continuous taste of bile in his mouth, he found little time to enjoy the irony.

The nurse walking along with him seemed to have little time to enjoy anything.

". . . And multiple skull fractures," she finished, the last in a long list of afflictions Salim was suffering from. "We haven't determined the internal damage to the organs."

"But is he going to be all right?" Heller asked.

"You'll have to ask the doctor," she said, leafing through a clipboard of information. "Did you actually see the fight?"

"Fight?"

"The fight in the bar—it says here he got caught up in some sort of brawl. . . ."

Heller considered his options, thought better of it. "Can I see him, please?"

The nurse skimmed the information given, form after form.

She motioned for Heller to follow her.

* * *

Most of the patients were by themselves, alone.

It was a large, cavernous room, walls lined with identical cots, each one witness to different states of pain, sickness, and anguish. Scattered movements from nurses, doctors, and a select amount of visitors.

Heller glanced at the beds as he passed, trying his best to keep up with the nurse.

Closed eyes and open ones. All pleading and immediate, whether awake or in dreams.

They arrived at Salim's bed.

Heller felt his stomach turn.

Salim's face was almost completely covered in bandages, gauze wrapped around his wrists, neck brace hugging him in an undignified manner, close to insulting.

Officer McCullough was standing by, in full uniform, hat in his hands.

"Bike boy," he said, and Heller had to stop himself from lashing out before seeing Salim's eyes shift under swollen lids.

"You are all right," Salim sighed, voice parched and damaged.

"I told you he was all right," Officer McCullough said. He put a hand on Heller's shoulder. "He thought something had happened to you."

Heller shook McCullough off violently, kneeled down by Salim's side.

"I'm sorry," Heller said, speaking rapidly, worried Salim might die at any moment. "I'm sorry for what I said, I'm really sorry."

"Never be sorry . . ." Salim's speech was slurred, words more of a collage than actual sentences. "Never be sorry. This is good . . . this is good news. This is great news."

Heller balled his fists, stood up, and faced Officer McCullough.

"What's all this about a bar fight?"

Officer McCullough looked around, made sure there were no doctors nearby. "He's telling them it was a bar fight," he said quietly. "He's refusing to press charges—"

"Is *he* refusing to press charges?" Heller asked, enraged. "Did *he* say it was a bar fight? Or was it you? Is that what you're telling them so he *won't* press charges?"

"Look—"

"Look, I don't think it's that difficult to see what happened, and I think you *know* what happened. I don't think you have *any* place trying to speak on Salim's behalf. I don't even know why you're here—did Bruno send you over as insurance?"

Officer McCullough bristled. "That's some mouth you've got on you, bike boy."

"That's some badge you've got there, *officer*," Heller fumed. "You expect me to listen to your story while my friend dies because of *you?*"

"Hey, listen!" McCullough whispered harshly. "You can't assume things are like that."

"Like what?"

"I'm an officer of the law. I've been on the force since I was twenty-five—my father was an officer—and don't think I follow my badge blindly or abuse it like that asshole Bruno. I know what goes on, I know what happened to

Salim, and I know *that* is not what I do. I see the young recruits—they go through training faster than I can fill out a report, and it's hit or miss whether they're taking the job for the virtue or the power. I love what I do, it's my job, and officers like Bruno make me *sick*, but I've been doing this for too long to try to fight it. . . ."

McCullough took a breath, composed himself. "I'm aware of the faults and I do everything I can to work around them. Don't think for a moment that I don't know about Salim and that by law he shouldn't be in this country. My grandparents immigrated from Ireland, and I've never forgotten what they had to go through. I'm here to serve and protect anybody who needs it, regardless of a meaningless document, and it was *Salim's* decision not to press charges. He's telling everyone it was a bar brawl because he doesn't believe in the justice of man; he lost faith in it a long time ago. So don't think you have any more right than me to speak on his behalf."

"And you won't speak out against Bruno?" Heller asked.

"I can't change anything from within. Nobody can, it's too large a problem. . . . And I'm old, bike boy. I'm tired. I did the best I can, and I'm not proud when I see things like this, but I believe that what *I* do is right. And all I can do at this point is hope others will do right by me. But don't tell me this is my fault. . . . I'm an officer. It's my job. And Salim is my friend."

The air went out of Heller, shoulders slumped.

McCullough put an arm around him. "I want things to be different, too."

"Can we do anything?" Heller asked, eyes to the tiled floor, white and impartial.

Officer McCullough motioned to Salim.

Heller felt a hiccup in his chest. He nodded.

McCullough put his hat back on and walked out of the room.

chapter thirty-seven

Salim was sleeping fitfully.

Heller wished he could sleep, his fifth hour by Salim's bed stretching out into the sixth. Just about every patient in the ward was asleep, the activity of the day forgotten. Except for the occasional groan or cry, their silence filled the ward, floor to ceiling.

A nurse walked up to Heller, snapping gum in her mouth.

"I'm sorry, but visiting hours are over."

"I'm not visiting," Heller told her, his own words distant, removed from conflict. "I'm staying."

The nurse saw that she couldn't move him; nothing would.

She continued her patrol and left Heller and Salim alone.

3:00 a.m.

Heller walked slowly, taking careful steps along the rows of beds. He observed every face, watched each patient sleep. Broken limbs, shattered knees, shattered lives, the isolation of sickness. The nearly dead, the hidden. Trying to comprehend the sorrow he had been representing for so long. The other half of his messages. The source of his paycheck, the ruined lives that made it possible for Dimitri to have digital cable installed in his office.

He wandered, moonlight carpeting his movements.

Bodies everywhere.

Heller stopped in front of an old man attached to a respirator. His face was worn with age, lines in his skin tracing freeways and side streets.

Hospital-issued pajamas.

In his hand was an ambiguously light green card.

4 x 8.

Heller stood in front of him, seeing his breath count down minutes. . . .

Transfixed.

He slowly reached out his hand, reached for the card in the old man's hand.

The old man woke up, no movement other than his eyes snapping open, and saw Heller standing over him. His grasp tightened around the card, almost crumpling it as he pressed it closer to his body, eyes alight, defiant.

Heller withdrew his hand.

The two looked at each other.

Time passed.

A loud moan from another bed broke the connection.

Heller backed away.

He returned to Salim's side, sat down by him.

"Heller . . ." Salim was awake. His eyes were filled with warmth and he motioned for Heller to come closer. "I feel like shit."

Salim smiled, chuckled, coughed lightly.

Heller smiled, gave it his best attempt, at least.

"You're going to get better," Heller said, trying to sound reassuring. "We'll get you out of here."

"I'm good at getting out," Salim said, neck taut with the effort of speaking. "I'm good at escaping. . . ."

"I don't mean escape," Heller said. "I mean—"

"I escaped from prison," Salim said, eyes large with a sense of self-wonder. "You don't know what those places are like, but I made it out. . . . And I escaped from Nizima's valley before they could take me back there. . . . Always moving . . . Nobody catches me."

He nodded off, fell asleep for a few seconds, then woke up, kept talking.

"My father was from Troy. . . . First, I escaped the burning city. . . . I crossed the sea. My father had told me to build another city. . . . The queen of Carthage tried to stop me, she wanted . . . me. Dido wanted to keep me, they all wanted to stop me, but the gods said . . . no. You were waiting for me. . . ."

Salim's eyes asked for something beyond Heller's grasp. "Do you understand?"

Heller felt his throat contract. "I'm trying."

"Now the city is burning again. The city is always burning. . . ." Salim brought Heller close. "If I cannot escape . . . If I cannot escape the burning city this time . . . it will be your turn. . . . This time, you must stay. One of us must stay. . . ."

Salim took hold of Heller's hand. "Do you understand?"

"Yes," Heller said, suddenly tired, laying his head down next to Salim.

It was surprisingly easy to sleep that night.

chapter thirty-eight

Heller was dreaming of a city slowly sinking into the sea when the gentle voice of the nurse seeped into the roar of the ocean:

"You have a visitor. . . . Hey. You have—"

A hand jerked at his shoulder, and in one jarring motion the collapse of a city was replaced by white walls, early sunlight. Heller was pulled to his feet, spun around, face to face with Dimitri Platonov.

An angry Dimitri Platonov, who gave him a gruff hug, pressing him close.

Apparently, vodka had a scent as well as a taste.

Dimitri broke away, grabbed Heller by the shoulders.

"You little bastard! I call the police stations looking for you and Officer McCullough tells me you're in the goddamn hospital!"

Heller was still adjusting, one foot stuck in his dream. "Dimitri, where did—?"

"I thought you had finally gotten it on that bike. Your father would have killed me! And I would have let him!"

"Sir." The nurse stood by, unsure. "You're going to have to lower your voice."

"I'm fine, Dimitri," Heller assured him, voice hoarse. "And I know what you owe my father, so I'll say it again. I'm fine."

"I know you're fine," Dimitri whispered harshly. "I can see that now, I'm not blind. But you may not be next time. I've told you I want you off that bike. If we weren't still short staffed, I would suspend you until you got yourself a pair of Rollerblades. . . . But I can't."

Dimitri straightened up, motioned toward Salim. "This your friend?"

Softly: "Yes."

"Can I count on you today?"

Heller looked at the nurse.

"There's not much you can do here," she said.

Long silence.

Heller raised his eyes, met Dimitri's. "What have you got for me?"

Dimitri held up an ambiguously light green card.

4 x 8.

"Elsa Martinez," Dimitri began. "Her husband died of a heart attack. He was young, and it was abrupt, so I'm not entirely sure she'll be expecting it. Be sure and come back right afterward so we can clear up the rest of your assignments at the office. . . . And where the hell is your Soft Tidings shirt?"

Heller looked down, realized he was still wearing the white shirt Magaly had given him. He looked up at Dimitri.

"On second thought," Dimitri said, "I really don't want

to know. Just take care of Elsa Martinez. . . . That flower thing you do? I would pick out something extra for this one—something special . . . on me."

He held up some money, folded and green.

Heller took it out of his hands without a word.

chapter thirty-nine

It was a beautiful day. Perfect balance of sunshine, cool breeze from the water making things right, and even the trees seemed to smile for once, leaning down with approval as Heller chained his bike to one of them.

Hair a mess, clothes in need of a good wash.

Heller held a bouquet of flowers in one hand, his note in the other.

He looked up at the Lower East Side building.

Narrow stairs.

The doors were numbered randomly, skipping from three to fifteen to nine to eleven.

Heller plodded up and down, trying to organize it all, finally coming to number sixteen. "Elsa Martinez," he mumbled, checking his card. "Apartment sixteen."

That was the one.

Heller readied his flowers, assumed a professional poise, knocked.

Footsteps, the sound of locks being undone.

The door opening.

Silvia was there.

Gray shirt and cutoff shorts, not her work clothes.

Then again, she wasn't at work. . . .

She was there. . . .

Heller's surprise mirrored hers.

Silvia cocked her head, trying to understand.

Heller understood all too well—it all came together far too obviously and he kept his mouth closed, jaw locked.

Someone had died and Silvia had no idea.

It was a Tuesday.

Silvia saw the flowers, smiled.

"Flowers . . . ," she observed. "Better than cake. And certainly better than a bike."

Heller gave her a freakish smile.

"So did you ask around about me?" Silvia asked, mock accusation. "Someone tell you that I love flowers? More than just about anything. Is that what you were told?"

Heller kept smiling, face hurting.

"Hey," Silvia said. "I thought I knew you! You helped me out with the stamps that one day at the post office. . . . Hey, that's right! Guess what?"

Meekly: "What?"

"I got a letter yesterday—someone who knows my father told me that he may be coming to the city! I'm going to get to see my father again!"

Heller snapped out of his trance, suddenly returning to the wrong side of reality.

He couldn't be there as a messenger.

There was nothing to tell.

Nothing wrong with the world other than an ambiguously light green card in his hand.

He stuffed it into his back pocket, extended the flowers, said:

"Congratulations."

Silvia took the flowers. "Thank you."

"It's your day off."

"Yes."

"And you're alone? Your mother . . . isn't in?"

"No."

"Do you want to go out?" Heller blurted. "With me? To celebrate? The two of us?"

Silvia looked a bit taken aback.

"Yes," she said, surprised at her own response.

Silvia closed the door in Heller's face.

Heller waited, out of sorts.

The door reopened, and Silvia was standing there with a strange look on her face, not entirely sure why she was doing what she was doing. She gave a small, airy laugh and held up a set of keys:

"I had to get my keys."

"All right."

They walked out into the daylight, out onto the sidewalk. The two of them side by side, past Heller's bike. He watched it as they went on by. Glanced back a second time. Heller and Silvia kept walking, returning to their defensive states, conversation taking on the form of early seconds in a boxing match: a slow circling, cautious moving, exploratory jabs.

". . . Do you like food?" Silvia asked.

"I guess . . . ," Heller said, corrected himself. "I mean, I know I like food, yeah."

"Lunch, I meant lunch. Do you like lunch?"

"Yes . . ." Heller glanced back at his bike again. "Maybe we could get some. Get some lunch."

"I forgot to eat breakfast."

Heller nodded, didn't further the conversation. He looked back at his bike one last time, its silver frame helplessly tied to the tree, a sad look on its front headlight.

"Hey," Silvia said.

"Yes?"

"Let's go this way," she said, motioning with her head.

They hung left, finally rounding a corner and into the unknown.

chapter forty

It was a strange day.

Something about it. Walking down the street and noticing that everyone is dressed in blue; rare moments when rain falls without the aid of a single cloud; something right on the tip of the tongue that seems to make faces at the usual without being noticed. It was something like that, and Heller felt it, knew Silvia did too.

They were sitting on MacDougal Street, outside of Yaragan—a hole-in-the-wall joint that served rapidly prepared Middle Eastern food. Not knowing what else to do, Heller had taken her there, thinking of Salim, hoping it might help break the ice. He bought them both falafels. Their only conversation since leaving her apartment had been Heller warning her not to put too much hot sauce on her falafel, which she ignored, dousing the pita pocket in red.

And now the two sat on the curb, a stone's throw from Creole Nights, the bar Salim had taken Heller to three days before. Its lights off, relaxing for the day.

The two ate quietly, each one trying to chew more softly than the other.

Silvia was shy but seemed to be imbued with a certain life confidence that Heller kept trying to tap into silently. They were almost done eating when Silvia finally spoke.

"What are these called?"

"Falafels."

"I've never had one. They're good." She took a sip of water. "Spicy."

"You shouldn't have put so much hot sauce on it."

"Oh, I like spicy. I like spice, makes things better."

Heller felt as though he had just lost a contest. He went back to saying nothing, hoped that he might accomplish more that way. He took a bite of his falafel, and some white sauce ran down his hand. Still chewing, he tried to wipe it off before Silvia could notice.

"Do you go to the movies at all?" Silvia asked.

"I don't like movies," Heller said, mouth full. He swallowed. "There's a few, I guess, but nothing worth ten dollars."

"I know. I wish they weren't so expensive, then I could go."

Wishing he knew more about media, Heller decided to see if he could keep up appearances. "Do you listen to music?"

"I don't know if you've heard of the music I listen to. . . ." She licked some white sauce off her hand. "Have you heard of Inti-Illimani?"

"Of course," Heller said, puzzled.

"I can't believe it." Silvia sounded relieved at some common ground discovered. "I love them."

"Them?"

"Their music."

Heller saw there was something very wrong. "Inti-Illimani is a volcano in Bolivia."

"I was talking about the Chilean music group."

"Oh . . . I guess I haven't heard of them. . . . I don't listen to music very much. . . . I've heard of the volcano."

Silvia looked as though she was about to ask if he was joking.

Heller searched the streets, looking for something to distract her.

His eyes, narrowed, saw a familiar face walking up the steps from Creole Nights.

"Lucky!" Heller called out.

Lucky glanced around, swaying slightly, saw Heller, cut across the street, almost into the path of a speeding car. He approached them, unshaven, eyes half shut to filter out the sun. A cigarette hung from his lips. The smell of whiskey wafted into the air with the smoke. "Hey, man," he said, "you should have come down to see us—we missed you."

"I didn't know you were open . . . ," Heller said, relieved to be talking to someone too drunk to find fault in everything he said.

"Actually, they're just closing up. Zephyr keeps the bar alive after hours sometimes. Well, most nights anyway. Who's your friend?"

"Silvia," Heller said. "Silvia, this is Lucky."

"Hey, Silvia."

"Hi, Lucky."

"Lucky's also Chilean," Heller said, hoping to impress Silvia.

"I'm not Chilean," Lucky mumbled. "Today I'm a French flight attendant."

Heller and Silvia were speechless.

"You look tired," Heller managed. "Maybe you should get some sleep."

"Sleep is for pussies," Lucky announced. "I'm off to happy hour, then maybe sleep . . . dream myself a woman I can look forward to lying next to every night."

He gave a half-wave salute and trudged away.

Silvia watched him go, the opposite of enchanted. A moody sadness seeped into her features.

"That's some mouth Lucky's got," she said, disapproving.

Heller prepared himself for an explanation, ready for her to wonder at how Heller had come to know such a . . . loser.

Instead, she found it in herself to backtrack.

"So you don't like movies. You don't listen to music. . . . What do you do?"

"I work for Soft Tidings."

"The message company?"

"You've heard of it?"

"Do you know Rich Phillips?"

Heller struggled with a mouthful of pita, suddenly dry and heavy. He swallowed with difficulty. Pretended to be indifferent.

"You don't like him, do you?" Silvia asked.

When Heller didn't answer, she took the slack. "Well, I don't think many people do. . . . He's like that, I suppose. He has a way that's difficult to understand. . . . But I think he's nice." Silvia noticed Heller's intense stoicism. "My only problem with him is that I don't find him very attractive. . . ."

She darted her eyes askance to see Heller's reaction. Heller did the same—but not in time to catch Silvia in the act. It went back and forth a few more times. . . .

Heller let the faintest smile spread across his face as he took another bite of falafel.

chapter forty-one

Heller and Silvia strolled through Central Park between patches of shade and sunlight. Silvia looked at everything with interest, eyes observant and careful. Heller looked at her as often as he could, still amazed he was walking with this girl through the park, amazed that a light wind from the reservoir found time to blow small flower petals into their path.

Silvia had a bit of white sauce on her lip. Heller still hadn't found a reasonable way to tell her.

"I thought you messengers wore Rollerblades, bike boy."

"I'm saving my money," Heller said dismissively.

"Saving for what?"

"Well . . ." Heller saw a group of ducks staring at him from a nearby pond. They made him nervous, and he tried to steer the walk in a different direction. "It's complicated."

"I'm sure it isn't as complicated as you think. . . ."

"It's strange, though. . . ."

"You can tell me. . . ." She stopped her stride, looked up

at him through a few strands of hair. "You gave me flowers, remember?"

Heller looked down at her, noticed she had long eyelashes. Her face beamed up at him, and he knew that if he didn't start talking, he might be forced to try something else, and with the lesser of two risks very clear, Heller told her.

"In 1904 a young man by the name of Henri Cornet won the Tour de France. Now, most of the competitors in the Tour de France are young men. The oldest to ever win was thirty-six-year-old Firmin Lambot in 1922. I say Henri Cornet was a young man in particular because he was the youngest cyclist to ever win the Tour. . . ."

Silvia stared at Heller, whose body seemed to be growing with the release of his story, his words coming quicker, effortless and unrehearsed.

"And back in 1904, the Tour de France was about as dirty as sports could get. Two thousand five hundred kilometers over nineteen days, and no chance for sleep. Spectators would throw rusty nails in front of the tires of the competitors they didn't like, men would run each other off the road, and low regulation standards gave contestants the opportunity to sneak off the track and take a bus or a train. . . . Henri Cornet had to endure all of this, and he won in 1904. Now, ask me what the interesting part is. . . ."

"What's the interesting part?" Silvia asked, fascinated.

"In 1904 it wasn't a big deal that Henri Cornet was the youngest to win the Tour, because the first Tour de France was in 1903. Being the youngest to win in the second Tour meant nothing. It would be like Bill Clinton setting a world record for being the most forty-second president ever. No, the interesting thing is that as the years have gone by, Henri Cornet continues to be the youngest man to win the Tour. . . ."

Heller paused, almost as amazed at his own information as Silvia was.

"It's coming up to a century and the record remains uncontested," he continued. "I'm going to beat that record and be the youngest cyclist to win the Tour de France—and then I'm going to win six straight years in a row, beating Miguel Indurain's five-year streak, and if Armstrong beats the record before I get a chance to, I'll just have to win seven in a row. I'm going to race in more tours than Joop Zoetemelk, you can bet I'm going to beat Greg LeMond's time trial by a good two kilometers per hour, and once everyone thinks that's it for me, I'm going to bump Firmin Lambot out of his seat and become the oldest fart to ever win the Tour de France. . . ."

Heller was done. Out of breath as though he had just actually set all the records he had spoken of. Out of breath because he had never whispered a word of this to anyone. He felt lighter, shoulders loose, hands outside his pockets.

Silvia stood fast, in awe of his wildly optimistic ambition. She blinked and took in a breath, let it out, and asked:

"Do you shave your legs?"

"What?"

"Bikers shave their legs. . . . Do you shave yours?"

Heller didn't answer. Just as he was about to, Mrs. Chiang walked by with a basket of flowers, light shawl draped over her shoulders. "Soft Tidings to you, my friend," she greeted him, continuing on her way.

Heller waved, still high off his own rambling.

Silvia saw the exchange, raised her eyebrows. "Who was that?"

"Mrs. Chiang. I delivered her a message once."

"Do you mind if I tell you something?"

"No."

She cocked her head to the side, observing him. "You're a bit crazy, I think."

Heller was moved by this, felt a gentleness in how she said it.

"Thank you . . ." He smiled, put a finger on his mouth. "You have a bit of white sauce on your lip. . . ."

Without a trace of embarrassment, Silvia wiped all trace of white sauce from her mouth with the back of her hand. "What did you say those falafels were made from?" she asked.

"Chickpea. They're made from chickpea."

"Oh . . . well, then, you have a bit of chickpea stuck between your teeth."

Heller picked at a tooth.

"No, not that one . . ." Silvia directed him, miming his movements. "Not that one . . . the other one . . . there."

"All right?"

"Fine . . ."

A lengthy silence followed. Both looked like they were about to say something, waited for the other, waited as the ducks from the pond waddled past, honking encouragements.

Silvia gave a nervous laugh, brushed some hair out of her face.

"Inti-Illimani is a volcano in Bolivia?" she asked.

"Yes."

"How do you know that?"

"Uh, my parents built a clinic in the highlands of Bolivia. . . ." Heller scratched the back of his neck, voice losing some of its fullness. "My parents travel. They're like missionaries. Not in the name of religion or anything, just people on a mission, you know . . . Good people—it's just that I hardly ever see them anymore. But I used to travel with them. . . ."

Heller let his eyes rest on some distant point in the park, trying to appear casual.

"Do you miss them?" Silvia asked.

"Yeah," Heller said. "But they do good. My father, he does a lot of good. . . . It'd be nice to see them more, though. Africa's far away."

"Have you been?"

"When I was younger, yeah."

"What's it like?"

"It's not here. . . . I wish it were—there wouldn't be any reason for them to go."

"I'm sorry."

"I must have seen the sun rise in over fifty different places in my life." Heller sighed. "I think that's how I know the things I do."

Silvia stared at him. "Someday," she said softly, "you should take me someplace you've never been."

Heller thought about it. "I've never been to Troy."

"Let's go there today. . . . Can we go there today?"

"Hmm." Heller looked to the west. "I think we can."

They resumed their walk, even steps relaxed.

chapter forty-two

There were only a few people in the museum. Heller and Silvia wandered through the exhibits at their own pace, taking their time, an hour passing without notice. They made their way through a room of Greek art displaying Trojan themes. The air-conditioning ran silently, and their footsteps echoed up and over everything.

"Paris was willing to take Helen back to Troy," Heller was explaining in the hushed tone of museum speak, "but he refused to fight."

"He was a pussy," Silvia clarified.

Heller was shocked to hear it coming from her.

"That's some mouth you've got," he observed.

"Sorry," she apologized. "I didn't mean to offend you."

"No, no offense taken, I don't mind," Heller assured. "You just didn't seem to take it so well when we were talking to Lucky earlier."

"I don't like drunks. . . ."

She didn't say anything past that. Her face was set hard, unmoving.

"So you hate drunks. That's all right," Heller said.

"Anyway." Silvia waved off the topic with her hand. "It doesn't matter; Paris was a pussy if he couldn't step up to a mess he made."

"He couldn't take responsibility for his actions."

"Didn't the gods determine everything anyway?"

"Do you know the only thing Zeus feared?"

"Tell me."

"Fate." Heller gestured to the artwork around them. "The gods had their own fate to contend with, even as they controlled the destiny of human affairs. And what it came to was this: Troy was destroyed. Odysseus thought of a wooden horse and that one idea toppled an empire. And the gods had every right to be afraid, because one of the only people who survived was Aeneas, who went on to found Rome . . . and Rome replaced Aphrodite with Venus, Hermes with Mercury, and Zeus was replaced by Jupiter."

Silvia listened carefully.

"It all repeats itself," Heller said. "And there doesn't seem to be any stopping it."

"It's all destiny to you?"

"The other day someone told me that Chance is Destiny's best friend."

Silvia stared into space, pondered. Then: "I'm not sure I understand," she said apologetically.

Heller shrugged. "There's a lot I don't understand."

They smiled at each other.

"Hey, man."

Heller and Silvia glanced over to a doorway, drawn by the source of a third voice.

Benjamin Ibo was leaning against the frame in a museum security outfit.

"Beautiful woman," he said, his eyes on Silvia.

Silvia turned her head, bashful, trying not to smile too widely.

Benjamin didn't say another word. He extended his arms, inviting them into a separate room. Silvia and Heller walked in slowly, past Benjamin, who pointed to a glass case in a silent suggestion to take a look.

It was a Yoruba divination board, carved into stone. On it was a carving of a strange-looking creature. Heller and Silvia took in all the detail, transfixed. The museum had suddenly become empty, not another person in sight.

Heller turned back to look at Benjamin.

Benjamin nodded toward the creature on the divination board:

"Eshu . . ."

Heller turned back to stare at Eshu, remembering the mirror in his bedroom only yesterday.

Only yesterday, and the words ran around in Heller's mind, leaving trails to be followed, slowly growing more complicated, and eventually losing themselves in their own wake.

"How is your friend?" Benjamin asked.

"What?"

"Salim," Benjamin repeated. "Is he all right?"

Silvia looked up at Heller, a silent question hanging in her eyes.

chapter forty-three

Salim had slipped into further delirium.

Heller was standing with Silvia in front of the bed. His hand was on Salim's forehead, hot to the touch, slick with sweat. Silvia toyed with her fingers, fidgeting.

"How are you feeling?" Heller asked.

"Ah, yes . . ." Salim's eyes had lost focus, earned a larger depth. "I see you have found Nizima."

"Salim," Heller said with great effort, "this is Silvia."

"Hello, Salim," Silvia said politely.

"Nizima," Salim said to her. His eyes shifted to Heller. "She is so perfect. . . ."

Silvia blushed.

Heller watched Salim's lip tremble, felt his heart empty, tight chest and throat.

"I'm so happy she's here . . . ," Salim told him. "Aeneas escaped from the burning city to Rome. And he found you. . . . I'm so happy Nizima has found you again. She's home. She came to see you. . . . Make this her home. . . ."

Salim took their hands, put them together.

Heller and Silvia wrapped their fingers around each other instinctively.

"Thank you both, young lovers. . . ." Salim laughed, turned serious in a second. "Mmm . . . Thank you both. . . ."

Heller felt Silvia's thumb run against his hand.

"You will remember . . . ," Salim said.

Heller didn't have a chance to say anything else.

He watched Salim fall back into slumber.

Heller knew what he had to do from the moment the nurse pulled him aside to speak with him, to ask his relationship to the patient. Silvia hovered nearby as he tried to answer the questions. The nurse explained that they couldn't attend to Salim's needs without knowing who was paying for it, where they would get the money to run new tests. Heller listened, nodded.

"I have money," he told the nurse.

"Just as long as you—"

"I have money."

"There still wouldn't be a guarantee we can save him."

Heller thought of Salim trapped in that body.

"Do you accept checks?" he asked.

Silvia watched him closely as the nurse pulled a pen out of her breast pocket and directed them to reception.

chapter forty-four

Night had fallen on the city.

Sunlight asphyxiated, a dotted skyline replaced the sky.

Heller and Silvia were walking by the waterfront along the West Side Highway. The Hudson River meandered along, small-scale waves lapping against the concrete base of the promenade. Across the body of water, New Jersey lights shone in a miniature reflection of Manhattan. A giant illuminated clock as big as a building showed the time to be 9:15. Statue of Liberty on the horizon. Joggers and cyclists hurried past, a few dog walkers, couples out to taste the water in the air.

Silvia's arm was locked with Heller's, the two of them pressed close, evening winds coming in from the south, where the World Trade Center stared down at them. Everything was almost as it should be, the already present ghost of Salim still hanging between them.

"Do you actually have enough money to cover for Salim?" Silvia asked.

"At least for a few days," Heller guessed. "He won't be needing surgery, so there's a bit of money saved."

"You really should—"

"The Grand Tour can wait," Heller told her.

"Are you—?"

"The Tour de France can wait."

They continued in silence, down to Battery Park City.

A boat sailed by, giving a little more churn to the steady stream of water.

Heller and Silvia stopped. Leaned against the metal railing and watched the vessel cross paths with another craft. Silvia slipped her arm back around Heller's and kept her eyes out over the water.

"Who's Nizima?" she asked.

"Salim is in love with her," Heller said. "She married someone else. Back in Turkey."

"That's sad."

Heller agreed silently.

"I miss my father," Silvia told him.

"Look, Silvia, I—"

"He wanted me to ride a bike," Silvia said, voice projecting backward, beyond the city, somewhere else. "Wanted me to learn, anyway. I think I wanted to also, I'm not sure. So he put me on this bike, an old one, not like yours. It used to belong to him. . . . I tried to pedal a few times and I fell."

"The scar on your knee?" Heller asked, voice hoarse.

"The scar on my knee . . ." Silvia took a moment, then: "When my mother came to the hospital, I did that thing. I blamed my father, that he pushed me too hard."

Heller was beginning to tense, torn between wanting to hear her story and wishing she could let it go, change the subject.

"My father's a gambler," she explained. "And a drinker . . . *un perdido*, that's what my mother always called him."

"*Un perdido?*" Heller asked, butchering the pronunciation.

"Scoundrel. Someone who's lost. A loser . . . And he was, but he never . . . mistreated me. He was a good father to me. And when I told my mother about the bike . . . that was it. She snuck us out of Santiago. Illegally. Divorce is against the law there, and for a parent to leave the country with their child they needed, still need signed documents from the other parent. We went to Miami, then moved here after a few years—so he wouldn't find us. . . . I miss him. . . . He was the only person who could really make me laugh. He'd make faces. . . ."

Heller could feel her regret, the loss of her father, knew more about it than she did, knew what it was that had managed to bring them both to be standing at the water's edge, together. He watched her eyes kiss the water. Reached into his back pocket and pulled out the card from Soft Tidings. Silvia didn't notice him standing on the edge of that cliff, thought he was still there with her.

"Silvia—"

"Hey, the messenger!"

Walking through the park was Christoph Toussaint, arm in arm with Magaly DuBois.

Heller froze in his resolve.

Magaly stared at him.

After all, Heller was wearing her shirt.

"Beautiful woman!" Christoph called out, pointing to Silvia and continuing along his way.

Heller quickly shoved the card back in his pocket before Silvia could see it.

"Word on the street is you're a beautiful woman," he told her.

"How do you know all these people?" Silvia asked in wonder.

"My job."

"It must be difficult giving those messages."

"... Yeah."

Silvia sighed. "What's it like?"

"It—" Heller found himself actually thinking about what it was, and he had trouble choosing his words. "It makes me happy. I don't know why, but . . . It's a moment I look for in the faces of the people I deliver to. Like there's some truth to be found there. Something real. More than what surrounds us, the hubbub, noise, billboards, magazines, and television screens—something . . . honest."

"Is that how you feel on the bike?"

"The entire world . . ." Heller's voice was uneven, pressing past his lips. "I feel that people could, in another life possibly, be capable of so much. When I'm on my bike, it's the only time I feel like there's anything to . . . be faithful about. To have faith in something. I just always feel . . . isolated."

Heller looked at Silvia, saw the sky in her eyes.

Silvia kissed him.

Softly, lips pressed lightly against his, only for the space of a second.

Heller couldn't take his eyes off her.

"I've been to Buns 'n' Things every day for the past six months," he confessed in a voice barely audible.

"I wish I had seen you there," Silvia told him.

"There's other things . . ."

Silvia started to laugh, an edgy giggle.

"What?"

"Buns 'n' Things," she said. "I just realized what a stupid name that is. . . ."

She continued to giggle.

Then she stopped and kissed Heller again.

A strong kiss, lips locked. The light touch of tongues, a somersault in their stomachs, lungs searching for a way to hold the air filling them. Heller felt himself, everything, the entire city fall apart in that kiss and build itself back up.

His imagination had been nowhere close to this.

Silvia broke away, eyes still closed, holding Heller tightly.

Their foreheads pressed together.

"Bike boy," she whispered, breathless, "what *is* your name?"

"Heller," he managed between inhalations. "Heller Highland . . . I work for Soft Tidings. We met earlier."

"I remember."

They kissed again, intense and unbelieving.

And again.

And again . . .

chapter forty-five

Streetlights continued to burn brightly, reflected in the water.

The hands of the giant clock across the Hudson had moved to one in the morning. Heller and Silvia could see it from the bench they were sitting on, their legs stretched out. Silvia was leaning against Heller. He held her, arms wrapped around her waist.

Content. Pleased. Perfect.

"I like being with you," Silvia told him.

"Me, you."

"You sound like Tarzan."

They lay there. A slow chill snuck in with the winds.

Silvia took Heller's hand and moved it to one of her breasts. He held his hand there, curious at the feeling.

"Do you like that?" he asked, mouth close to her ear.

"I like you," she whispered. "It feels nice. Comfortable . . . Do you like it?"

"Yes."

Silvia let out a slow breath, closed her eyes, breathed in, chest rising against Heller's palm.

"Silvia . . . ?"

"Mmm?" Silvia murmured dreamily.

"This was pure chance," Heller told her. "The strange thing about chance is that you can't understand it. Chance doesn't make any sense until it becomes destiny. . . ."

Heller continued to talk, more to himself, as it all came out of him.

"It's difficult, because there's a world of pain out there. And all people have to hold on to are memories or God, Allah, or . . . little wooden horses. I don't know what it is . . . but there's something."

Heller hesitated, scared. "I just know . . . I had a message for you. I really can't do this for much longer, be people's messenger, I know it now. And I'm sorry about your father. . . . I'm so sorry."

The clock had made its way to fifteen minutes past the hour.

Heller waited for Silvia's response, held his breath.

Her answer to it all was a light snore.

Silvia had fallen asleep.

Heller swallowed carefully, worried the movement might wake her up.

He sighed.

Kissed her hair.

The water kept on its course throughout all of it.

chapter forty-six

The blare of a police siren woke them up.

Heller and Silvia groaned, stirred, stretched.

The sun was rising, and Heller was once again wearing clothes well past their prime.

Silvia didn't seem to mind, and she kissed him lightly.

"Hi," she said, raspy.

"Hi."

They kissed again.

"I'll walk you home," Heller offered.

"I'll join you," Silvia said.

She kissed him again.

The two of them stood, muscles aching, feeling good.

Heller felt the air rush out of him all at once.

He took a few steps to where his bike had been chained a little less than twenty-four hours ago. Now there wasn't even a sign of the chain. Empty space.

"No," Heller said.

"Oh, no . . . ," Silvia echoed.

Heller looked around, a distant hope that th

ꞇmewhere in the vicinity. A few kids off to day camp,
ꞇr mother telling them where she would meet them
ꞇer. Some squirrels. That was all.

"My bike . . ."

Silvia put her hand on his shoulder.

Heller was in complete shock, unable to respond.

"Look," Silvia tried, "come up to my place. You can call
the police from there. We'll get your bike back. . . ."

She was saying the same thing at the entrance to her
apartment. "Heller? We'll find your bike. It's going to be all
right. . . ."

Heller nodded.

Silvia dug into her pocket, got her keys.

She opened the door, let Heller in.

Dimitri was there.

It was the second thing that struck Heller as the door
closed behind him. The first was that the apartment was
extremely bright. The blinds, if there were any, were
raised, and the sun seemed to be positioned directly outside. The walls were bright white, light reflecting off them,
not a single decoration to soften the glare.

Then there was Dimitri.

He was standing with a short, round woman with blond
highlights streaked in dark hair. She was somewhere
around her late thirties, and Heller didn't need an introduc-
tion to know that it was Elsa Martinez.

Silvia's mother.

Her eyes were dry, but the rest of her betrayed a state of
absolute distress.

Heller knew why, suspected Dimitri did as well, and
ꞇspected Silvia was about to find out.

"Dimitri," Heller said.

"Heller," Dimitri said.

"Silvia," Elsa said.

"Mother?" Silvia asked.

"Heller," Dimitri began again, face a blank slate of professionalism. "First of all, you're fired."

"Heller, who is this guy?" Silvia asked.

"My boss," Heller said.

"Ex-boss," Dimitri corrected. "What on earth is wrong with you, Heller? Not only do you disappear from work without a word's notice, but then I have to hear from Mrs. Martinez's family that they haven't received word about the message they sent!"

"What's going on?" Silvia asked, sensing the sudden change in her life going one step further than before.

Dimitri's eyes shifted to sympathy. "I'm sorry it had to be like this."

"Let me," Heller pleaded.

"No!" Dimitri shouted. "You don't work for me anymore!"

Heller turned to Silvia, rushed, trying his best to beat Dimitri to it. "Silvia, I was supposed to give you a message . . . and I didn't."

Silvia stepped back with an overwhelming dread masking her face. "What?"

"Your father is dead," Heller said, all at once. "He died of a heart attack. I was supposed to tell you yesterday, but I couldn't—"

"Get out," Silvia said.

"But I couldn't because I wasn't ready to."

"*Get out!*" Silvia screamed at him, pushing him toward the door, tears in her eyes.

"Silvia . . ."

"I can't believe what you've done to me."

She shoved him out the door and stood there, a nest of rage.

Heller tried to say something and the words wouldn't come.

"Heller—" Dimitri began.

"I know," Heller said, defeated.

Silvia's face contorted. She burst into tears and slammed the door.

Heller remained in the stairway, left alone. Listening to Silvia's sobs through the walls. Listened to her choking on the news of her father.

He made as though to knock, knuckles resting against the wood.

There wasn't anything he could do, and he took a few steps down toward the exit, trying to think of a way out of what had just happened.

A door opened, and Heller turned, hopefully.

It was another apartment door. A seven-year-old child looked out through the chained crack of the entrance to his home. Heller raised his hand in a halfhearted greeting, mouthed a hello.

The child closed the door.

Heller went outside. His bike was still gone.

It was Wednesday morning, and Heller had been sixteen for an entire week.

chapter forty-seven

The 6 train bounced and rattled on the rail, squeals of brakes and sparks illuminating the dark underground beyond the windows. The seats were packed, not even much standing room. Heat like a sauna, the smell of bodies packed together. Advertisements for cosmetic surgeons. Club Med retreats where the sands were white and water was clean and pure.

Heller sat between two construction workers, their wide shoulders pressing against him, jostling him with every sharp turn of the subway. Nobody glanced at anyone else. Eyes all downcast. Tired and sweating under their work clothes.

The door between cars opened, and a woman with a large stomach and a dirty maternity dress stepped in, a paper cup in one hand. Hair in clumped braids. Smudged face and lips chapped.

"Excuse me, people. I am sorry to interrupt your ride, and I hope you are having a pleasant day. . . ."

Nobody turned to look at her. They all knew where it was going.

"Ladies and gentlemen, I am seven months pregnant and I have no home. . . ." Her eyes were ashamed, voice a steady monotone of despair. "I have also lost my job. I do not want to be a bother, but I am hungry and I am worried about my baby, and I need a place to stay. . . ."

One by one, the passengers began paying attention. The woman had an indefinable quality about her. With every word, invisible strings pulled at heads, Heller's included, and by the end of her speech, he was entirely mesmerized, empathy unhinged and uncontrollable.

". . . All that I ask is for whatever you can find in your heart to spare: some change, a bit of food, an address for me and my baby to find help. I am alone and appreciate your kindness. God bless you. . . ."

Everyone's face remained hard and expressionless as she began her slow charity walk down the aisle. Still, just about everyone dug into their pockets, jingled change, dropped what they could into her cup.

"Thank you, God bless," she said with every donation. "Thank you, God bless. Thank you, God bless. Thank you, God bless. Thank you, God bless. Thank you, God bless . . . Thank you, thank you, God bless. God bless. Thank you, God bless . . ."

Heller had spent all but a quarter on his subway fare.

He dropped the twenty-five-cent piece into her cup, followed her with his eyes as she inched her way past the rest of the workaday world.

She exited the car, on to the next one.

The train continued to clatter through the tunnels.

Three minutes later, a grinding halt at the Twenty-eighth Street stop.

Heller stood. Popped out from between the two construction workers.

He stepped onto the platform, conductor on the speakers already asking for the rest of the passengers to stand clear of the closing doors. They chimed and slid shut and the train started up, racing to its next destination.

Heller lurched through the turnstile with excessive difficulty, energy drained.

Walked up the steps, out into the open air.

Down the block he saw the pregnant woman. She was standing in a doorway, reaching under her dress. Heller watched her give a few tugs and pull out a large plastic stomach from beneath the material. She slung it over her shoulder and continued on her way, a smooth stride in the legs, head held high, back straight.

Heller couldn't see the look on her face, but was sure that if he had, it would have been unrecognizable as the woman he saw in the subway.

The woman dissolved into a pack of schoolkids on a field trip.

Heller went the opposite way.

chapter forty-eight

The apartment seemed empty. Heller slammed the door behind him.

Leaned against it.

"Heller?"

It was Eric's voice. Coming from the kitchen.

"Yes," Heller answered.

"Come in here, please."

Heller went into the kitchen. Eric was seated at the table. Florence was leaning against the counter, momentarily halted in the act of cutting an apple. They both looked at Heller with their faces barely under control.

"Where were you?" Eric asked.

"I . . ."

"Where were you?" Florence insisted.

There was no way to explain.

"I know that we're only your grandparents," Eric went ahead, anger slowly coming out, "but the way you have been acting for the past few days is inexcusable, even to such incidental people as Florence and myself—"

"Silvia broke up with me."

"You're sixteen!" Eric shouted. He tried to calm down, managed with clear difficulty. "Sixteen! I don't care if Silvia broke up with you! Do you know what it's like to stay up all night wondering if your grandson is still alive?"

"Do you know what it's like to be *sixteen*?!" Heller burst out, body trembling. "Do you? It's a whole other world for us out there!"

"Don't talk to me about what it's like out there."

"I'll talk—"

"You don't know what Florence and I have seen, what your father and mother have seen. *You* don't know what it's like out there, you're a goddamn child!"

"Who cares what you've seen!" Heller yelled. "I don't need to see it to know that I don't want to inherit what you've left me! Any of it!"

"Well, you're getting it," Florence spoke up, cutting into the apple calmly. "Whether you like it or not, Heller. It's yours."

Heller opened his mouth to answer and saw the futility of it all. The futility of trying to explain, the futility of trying to understand. There was no debating anything, and it was clear nobody was going to win.

The refrigerator clicked, began to hum.

Eric, Florence, and Heller didn't take it any further.

Took it all in.

When the phone rang, everyone jumped, Florence dropping the knife to the floor. She stooped down as Heller went to pick up the phone, cutting it off in midring.

"Hello . . . ," Heller said, not recognizing the voice asking for Heller Highland. "Yes, this is him. . . ."

It was the hospital.

Heller's face darkened, and he was off the phone in less than a minute. He set the receiver back with a soft click.

Heller thought Eric and Florence must have seen the color drain from his face, heated flush replaced by a sick sort of white. They shifted instantly. Their hardness dissolved, the enforcers now replaced with Heller's grandparents, back again.

"What is it?" Florence asked.

"Salim is gone."

"Salim?" Eric was confused.

"Gone from where?" Florence asked.

"They say he left the hospital last night," Heller told them. "Nobody saw him go."

"Salim was in the hospital?"

"I have to go," Heller said.

He turned to leave, stopped in his stride by Eric's voice: "Heller . . ."

Heller didn't turn around. He could see them anyway, in that cozy kitchen, wearing their age on their faces, concerned stares second nature after so many years.

"I'm sorry," Heller said, sincerely wondering who he was talking to. "I'm just sorry for everything."

He ran out the door, down the stairs, and raced on foot to see if there was any possible way to find his friend in a city of millions.

chapter forty-nine

It wasn't a problem finding Salim's apartment building. Wasn't a problem getting in—the lock on the front door was still busted. Wasn't a problem entering the room—the door was unlocked.

Heller stopped at the entrance.

The entire place was empty. The cots were gone, clothes, scant decorations, even Salim's books. Vanished. All that was left were the cracks in the walls and the incessant dripping of a broken faucet in the bathroom.

"What are you doing here?" an accusing voice snapped behind him. A large woman in a polka-dot dress was poised in the doorway, gritty eyes and permanent grimace carved into her cheeks.

"Are you the landlady?" Heller asked.

"Land*lord*," she insisted, clearly wearing the title on her sleeve. "I'm the landlord, and this is my building."

"Where did everybody go?"

"They took off, disappeared last night." She peered at him accusingly. "You don't actually know those Arabs, do you?"

"They are *not*—" Heller caught himself, felt he might be in over his head. "No, I don't."

"You know it turns out they had no papers."

"I don't know anything," Heller said, aware that there was no need to lie to her. It was the honest-to-God truth. "I really don't."

He pushed past her, almost knocking her down.

"Hey!" she shrieked, calling after him as he bolted down the stairs. "You come back here again, I'm calling the cops, you little sneak! Get the HELL out of my place!"

She was still ranting when Heller hit the street.

In the reflection of a parked-car window, he caught a good look at himself. He was a total mess. The sidewalk on either side of him seemed to stretch out into infinity. Where to go, where to even start trying to make things right . . .

Heller felt his necklace rubbing against his neck.

He ran one block north, looked left, looked right, took in every angle of the intersection. On the adjacent corner were a couple of phone booths. Heller ran between the bumpers of gridlocked cars and picked up the first phone he got to. Its cord was severed. He tried the other one; the healthy sound of a dial tone. Heller reached into his pocket, remembered the woman in the subway.

Heller swore, slammed down the phone. At a loss, in a state of near delirium, he jumped into the middle of sidewalk pedestrians and announced:

"Excuse me, ladies and gentlemen!"

A few people turned, some even stopped, and Heller kept right on:

"I'm sorry to interrupt your walk, but I have just lost my job, my bike, my girlfriend, and possibly my best friend!

There is no way to fix this, but if anybody can find it in their hearts to spare a quarter, one quarter! I don't want to be a bother, but I don't seem to have any other option! GOD BLESS YOU ALL!"

Heller finished with his arms outstretched, chest heaving.

A lanky twenty-year-old with glasses and a gingery goatee walked up and dropped twenty-five cents in Heller's hand.

"Please," the charitable stranger said, "just promise you'll never do that again."

"I promise."

"Good." He winked and went on his way.

Heller went back to the phone, lifted the receiver.

He reached into his back pocket, searching for a phone number. Pulled out an ambiguously light green card, 4 x 8—the message for Silvia that should have been delivered by Heller. He crumpled it viciously and threw it to the floor. Reached back into his pocket and pulled out a business card.

Heller dialed with poor accuracy and had to try three times before finally getting a ring on the other end.

He found himself crossing his fingers, hoping for the first in a long string of miracles.

chapter fifty

Benjamin Ibo listened intently to the whole story.

Heller talked fast, knowing he was leaving out massive details. He held tightly on to the cup of coffee Benjamin had served him. Benjamin's apartment looked different from when he had appeared there on business two weeks ago. Nothing like the apartment he remembered. Transformed, purified somehow.

None of it comforted Heller, and he was done relaying the events to Benjamin in under fifteen minutes. Benjamin nodded, leaned over the table, and put a hand on Heller's shoulder.

"I'm glad you came to me with this," he said.

"I'm glad you were home." An uncomfortable laugh escaped Heller. "I really have *no* idea where I'm going."

"It's all right," Benjamin assured him. "This is where we begin."

He went into a separate room, came back with a phone book, and dropped it on the table with a loud smacking sound.

"How long have you been working at Soft Tidings, then?" Benjamin asked.

"Around three months, since before school ended."

"Three months," Benjamin said. "You must have helped a lot of people."

Heller shook his head. "I've tried."

"I think you've done more than that."

"I don't think so."

"I think you're wrong." Benjamin sat down, started to say something, changed his mind. "You know, I am not going to get into a battle of woes with you. I find the who-has-suffered-more game to be childish and ultimately undignified. It is for people who cannot handle their suffering or for people who feel that there is some fault in not suffering enough. But what I will say is that I have suffered, and I have witnessed suffering, and the only time I have ever accepted defeat was when there was truly nothing to do but harvest my own wounds in hopes that something better might grow out of them. If inaction is one's only option, fine. If not, then accept that you are being beaten up and *do not help life do its job*—it is doing fine without your help, wouldn't you say, Heller?"

Heller bit his lip.

"How good is your memory?" Benjamin asked, opening the phone book.

"Above average," Heller answered.

"That is what I thought," Benjamin said, pleased. He picked up a pen from the table, gave it a click. "Now tell me stories, Heller. Tell me stories about people who were once in trouble. And don't change any names. . . ."

Heller began with his first message, a man by the name of Raymundo Caneque, and Benjamin began to flip through the phone book.

This continued on through the morning and early hours of the afternoon.

chapter fifty-one

It was unbelievable, but it was happening.

Heller watched from his room, a crack in the door showing him the living room, slowly filling with every passing minute past five p.m. Clients from his past, friends of Salim, all gathering together, seated on the couch, foldout chairs, lined up against the wall. Mrs. Chiang, Christoph Toussaint, Velu, Durim Rukes, and countless others. The murmur of discussion was reminiscent of precurtain in an opera house, everyone expectant, waiting for the show to start.

Eric and Florence stood near the door, overwhelmed at how they had managed to get so involved with their grandson's life over the course of the past week, considering how little they had seen of him during that time.

"Did you know Heller knew this many people?" Eric whispered to Florence.

"I didn't even know there *were* this many people," she confessed.

Heller still couldn't bring himself to face them all, and he kept the door between himself and the meeting, which was about to get under way with a declaration from Benjamin Ibo.

"Can I get everyone's attention, please?"

The conversation died down, eyes focused on Benjamin, who stood at the front of the audience. He waited for silence before continuing, straight to the point:

"It is a damn large city, and we don't know how much time we have. There are a lot of us, which is good, but at the same time, we don't need to end up on any goose chases, so . . . I want to make it clear that all information, whether it be concrete or some kind of lead, should be brought first either to myself or to Officer McCullough."

The rumble of conversation peaked again at the mention of a police officer in their presence. McCullough stepped forward, away from the wall. He was dressed in slacks and a white button-down shirt. He raised his hand and cleared his throat. . . .

"I recognize a few of you here today. . . ." The room fell silent. "And while some of you might recognize me, I'm not here as a police officer. My first name is Patrick."

Silence.

"All right." Benjamin eased back into the saddle. "Now, we need to do this right. Everybody with a cellular phone, raise your hand."

Everybody's hand shot up immediately.

"Never mind," Benjamin conceded. "Let's just do this. Come to me or Patrick, and we'll divide you into your respective groups. . . ."

Nobody moved.

"Let's get out there!" Benjamin declared, and everything stirred into activity.

Heller closed the door. He wandered over to his window, the muted sounds of organizing at his back. He pulled out the picture of Silvia. An empty shade of blue passed through him, and he traced his finger over the flat features of her face.

His door opened.

"Hey, you coming?"

Heller slipped the picture into his copy of *Don Quixote* sitting on the windowsill.

He turned.

Rich Phillips was standing in the middle of his room.

Thermal shorts and Nike T-shirt.

"Rich . . . ," Heller said.

Rich Phillips surveyed the bike posters, models, and magazines. "Look at all this. It's no wonder you're the best."

"What are *you* doing here?"

"I came with Iggy."

"What's *he* doing here?"

"He came to help."

"And what are *you* doing here again?"

Rich shrugged. "Well, you don't have a cell phone, do you?"

Heller shook his head, wondering where this was all going.

"Of course you don't," Rich said. "You don't even have a set of Rollerblades."

"I do so have Rollerblades," Heller said defensively. "I keep them in my closet so I won't have to use them."

Rich gave a short laugh. "You actually have Rollerblades?"

"Take them, they're yours. . . ."

Rich walked over to the closet, opened it. He reached

in and pulled out Heller's blades, held them at arm's length like a pair of crusted socks.

He made a face. "You call these Rollerblades? These cheap bastards couldn't even coast down the Atlantic."

"Richard." Heller was nearing the end of his patience. "What's your point?"

Rich dropped the Rollerblades and gave an unconvincing shrug. "They told me out there that you might be getting a call from your parents. Since you can't be in two places at once, I left your grandparents my cell number. So we can do this and you don't have to worry about missing your call, seeing as how you're the only teenager in Manhattan without a cell phone."

"I don't really want to speak to my parents."

"Well, I think that's too bad."

"And I don't think you know anything about this," Heller challenged.

"Well, I don't see how I could—"

". . . Your parents aren't off to every corner of the world except your own—"

"My parents are dead."

Heller shut his mouth.

Rich put his hands in his pockets, unabashed and direct.

"When I was fifteen. Plane crash, if you can believe it. I know you of all people would know the statistical improbabilities of that, but . . . it happened. I was raised by my uncle."

Heller found his voice. "I didn't know that."

"Well, now you have something new to tell your parents when they call."

Heller looked at Rich Phillips, thought, *Rich Phillips is in my room.*

Rich coughed, took his hands out of his pockets, and straightened himself.

"And another thing," he told Heller. "Stop being such a goddamn pussy about everything." He turned to the door. "I swear to God, if your skin were any thinner, you'd be transparent, you little bitch."

"Richard?"

Rich looked over his shoulder.

"What are you doing here again?" Heller asked.

Rich felt in his pocket, came out with a cell phone. He tossed it to Heller.

Heller extended his arm, caught it.

"You tell anyone about me," Rich warned, "and you're a dead man."

Heller nodded.

Rich Phillips walked out of the room.

Heller went to his closet, pulled out a jacket, and followed.

chapter fifty-two

The entire day was spent looking for Salim.

Heller, Rich, and Christoph searched the streets most familiar to them. Velu and a few others wandered the East Village, making their rounds with the vendors. Some of them, on hearing about Salim, packed up their stands and joined in the search. A few patrons from Creole Nights cruised the bars and pubs, dragging out whatever information they could from the bottom of beer mugs and shot glasses.

Meeting places were set up, strategies revised, neighborhoods circled on maps as they spread themselves all over lower Manhattan. There was little time for Heller to wonder at it all. Just moments when it became clear what was happening, the amount of effort put into the rescue of one man. No poems to be written about it, epic stories to be passed down, no tributes, headlines, movies of the week.

The rest of the city never stopped as Heller and the rest refused to cease.

Night made itself known and it was time to take stock of the day.

* * *

Everyone gathered at Creole Nights.

Much-needed drinks distributed among the search party, tables all occupied, everyone exchanging notes, passing information on to Benjamin Ibo, who went from table to table gathering results. Patrick McCullough and others had turned in for the day. Everyone else compared schedules and was already planning to see who could look for Salim during what hours the next day.

Heller sat at the bar, drinking a Sprite.

So far, the day's endeavors had yielded nothing. He kept an ear tuned to the conversation around him. Mostly Heller just played with his straw, tried to stay awake.

"Hey, kid . . ."

Wanda the waitress was now behind the bar. She was wearing glasses that night, black-rimmed and wide, an intellectual flair added to the mix.

"How's it all going?" she asked, eyes curious.

"Not good."

"Sorry . . ." She shifted her stance, left hand on her hip, right arm across her stomach with her right hand resting on the left hand. "You want a drink?"

"I already have one. Thank you, though."

"No, no, no," she clarified. "I mean, do you want a *drink*?"

"I don't know. . . ."

"It'll warm you up."

"It's warm enough as it is."

"Inside," she said. "It'll warm you up inside."

And it sounded nice, Heller had to admit it to himself.

"What do you recommend?" he asked.

237

"Something in a Jack."

She set down two shot glasses and filled them with an amber glow.

They picked up their glasses and toasted silently.

Wanda took her shot and slammed her glass down on the bar.

Heller didn't drink his whiskey, only held it. He could smell the fumes and it reminded him of his first night with Salim. Seated in Creole Nights, drinking Lucky's whiskey and Cokes. It was all swimming in his drink.

"I shouldn't," Heller said, putting down his whiskey. "Salim says I shouldn't."

Wanda looked at Heller with deep understanding. She picked up his shot glass, tilted her head back, sending the sour mash down her throat. She set the glass down and took Heller's hand in hers, giving it a light kiss. . . .

"Problem solved," she said, and left him to his thoughts.

Heller walked up the steps leading out of Creole Nights.

He took the cell phone from his pocket and dialed a number Benjamin Ibo had looked up earlier, despite Heller's protests.

Heller put the phone to his ear.

"Hello?" came Silvia's voice.

Heller hung up, flipped the phone shut.

He closed his eyes.

The phone rang.

Heller's eyes snapped open, heart skipping a beat.

He extended the antenna, answered in as calm a manner as he could manage.

"Hello?"

"Heller?"

It was his father's voice. Even through the distortion, Heller recognized it.

"Dad . . ."

"How are you?"

Heller sat down on the steps of Creole Nights. "I'm all right. . . ." He didn't know what to say. "How are you?"

"Fine. Listen, I've only got a minute, it's hard to get a good connection here."

"Yeah, I'm on a cell phone. . . ."

Static for a second, then his father's voice again: "You got a cell phone?"

"No, it's Rich Phillips's phone."

"Who's Rich Phillips?"

Heller found himself breathing out more than in. "How's Mom?"

"She's fine. . . . Have you learned to use the Roller-blades we bought you?"

"Well . . ." Heller rubbed his face. "I'm getting there."

"Oh . . . all right, Heller."

A full thirty seconds of static before his father came back on the line: "I have to go, Heller. . . ."

"Me too."

"We'll be home soon, I promise."

"Okay."

"Take care of yourself."

"I will . . ."

"I love you."

"Me too."

A sudden flare of interference hissed into Heller's ear

and then nothing. The connection broken, he closed the phone and pressed it against his forehead.

The door to Creole Nights opened, jingle of a bell.

Benjamin looked up at Heller from the depths. "You all right, man?"

Heller closed his eyes, muttered a reply.

"You should get some sleep," Benjamin advised. "That's what you told me when we first met, when you told me about my mother's death."

"I'm fine."

"Heller . . ." Benjamin walked up the steps until he was face to face with Heller. "Most of us are done for today. I don't know how long this is going to take—could be days, so . . . get some sleep."

"We have work to do."

"Heller, you need to sleep."

Heller sighed. He *was* tired. The day was still running through his bloodstream and he could almost feel the two shots Wanda had taken on his behalf, his body on the verge of collapse. Nerves shot. Lids scratching against his eyes. "I'll see you tomorrow," he told Benjamin.

"Hey . . ." Benjamin held out a twenty. "Take a cab, Eshu. I don't want you falling asleep on the subway and waking up in the Bronx."

Heller was too worn out to protest.

He took the money and stepped to the curb.

Four taxis went by before one of them finally took pity and stopped.

chapter fifty-three

Heller didn't do as he was told.

Instead, he went down to Kenmare Street.

The office lamps were all turned off. Lights from the street and screen savers staved off the darkness, patches of brightness sprawled across the floor, walls, desks. The shadows slept along with the phones, their silence filling every possible space in the empty room.

Heller stood in the middle of it all, saying goodbye. He felt as though he must have been born in a place like this. Not a hospital, as he had always been told, but in the nerve center of events after closing time. The comfort of absolute stillness.

The door to Dimitri's office opened.

Heller turned.

He saw Dimitri standing in the doorway, holding a glass of transparent liquid. Dimitri didn't seem surprised to see him. Heller wasn't surprised, either, and it occurred to him that he had been expecting it.

"Hello, Heller."

"Hey, Dimitri . . ."

Dimitri wandered into the room. His steps were out of rhythm with the rest of him. He made his way to a desk in front of Heller and leaned against it with his back to the windows. Street light poured in behind him, hiding his face.

"So . . ." Dimitri's voice was as reasonable as Heller had ever heard it. "You want to tell me how you got in here?"

"I have my own set of keys," Heller said, holding them up. They glinted in the darkness.

"What about the combination lock?"

"Iggy told me the combination," Heller said. "Couple of months ago, actually."

"Kid's got a big mouth."

"The biggest."

They lapsed into silence. Dimitri took a sip of his drink, then set it down. Heller watched him swallow, and a bizarre idea came to him:

"So now that you're not my boss anymore, could I just, like, take your drink and pour it on your head without any consequences?"

Dimitri gave a pleased guffaw. "I wouldn't, if I were you. Never cross a Russian."

"Just wondering."

"Any particular reason you're here?"

"I came to clear out my desk."

"You don't have a desk."

"Huh . . ." Heller looked around the room. "No wonder it's taking so long."

"You don't have anything to take from here," Dimitri said, his words slurring a bit.

"Well, then I came to give these back," Heller said, placing his keys on a nearby desk.

"Put those back in your pocket," Dimitri told him, suddenly serious.

"What are you talking about?"

"I'll suspend you for a week out of respect for the dead," Dimitri said. "After that, you're free to come back to work."

Heller shook his head. "No, I'm not."

"Didn't you just hear me?"

"You'll be fine without me, Dimitri."

"We need you at this place, Heller."

"No, you don't."

Dimitri looked down at the floor.

"You really don't," Heller insisted softly. "So I'm leaving my keys. And don't worry about my father. I'll handle him."

Dimitri looked up, face still concealed. "One last favor, then?"

"Yeah?"

"Let me tell him. . . ." Dimitri sounded sad and relieved. He lifted his weight off the table and began walking back to his office. "Let me explain. I believe I owe it to him."

"I think you've done enough for my father," Heller called after him.

Dimitri paused, once again in the doorway, his back to Heller.

"I will have after I've talked to him," he said.

It was clearly the end of the conversation, and Heller didn't feel he had anything more to add to the abandoned office.

"Good luck, Heller," Dimitri said. "And close the door on your way out."

Dimitri closed his own door.

After another minute alone with his old workplace, Heller did the same.

chapter fifty-four

Heller slept. Absolute and bottomless sleep. Not a dream graced his unconscious. Complete unawareness. Non-being. The comforting absorption of detail into shadow. Nothing but the drumbeat of blood, his own breath ringing somewhere in the darkness, the sound of cells dividing, surrounded by a mattress of numb deprivation.

Freedom from exhaustion.

His grandmother's voice woke him up.

Heller stirred, released a light groan. He rolled onto his back, sheets and blankets cocooned around him. Through his eyelids, he knew something was wrong with the light filling his room.

"What time is it?" he asked, eyelids fluttering.

"It's two in the afternoon, dear," Florence said. "You've been asleep for about fifteen hours."

"Crap." Heller burped, sitting up. "I need to get in touch with Benjamin."

"You have a visitor, Heller."

"Huh?"

"There's someone here to see you," Florence said. "Young lady, very pretty."

Heller breathed in abruptly, snorting, wide awake.

"Yeah, all right." His eyes searched his room, looking for his pants—any pair of pants. "Tell her to come in, sure."

Florence walked out of the room, closed the door behind her.

Heller jumped out of bed and ran to his closet.

The Rollerblades fell from their shelf, bouncing off his shoulder in a sharp burst of pain. Heller shook it off, tore some pants from a hanger, and slipped them on, hopping around the room.

He zipped his fly just as the door to his room reopened.

Silvia walked in, paused when she saw him half-dressed, torso pale and skinny.

Heller kept stock-still, thinking the less he moved, the less chance there would be to blow this opportunity.

In Silvia's hand was a flower.

Carnation. Red.

Heller smiled. "Silvia . . . you're here. . . . Hi."

Silvia walked up to him, handed him the flower.

Heller accepted. His smile widened, and he leaned close to embrace her.

Silvia put up her hands.

"Stop it," she said, voice cold.

Heller froze. Silvia backed away slightly, face determined. She reached into her bag.

Pulled out an ambiguously light green card.

4 x 8.

"Rich was supposed to deliver this," she began flatly. "He said he couldn't do it. I'd been to the offices looking for you. So I volunteered."

Heller was filled with a golden dread.

"What are you talking about?" he asked.

" 'Dear Eshu.' " Silvia read from the card, delivering her words with as much detachment as she could. " 'After all the comfort you have brought me, I wish I could do the same for you. I am so sorry to tell you that our dear Salim Adasi is no longer with us. He was found dead under the Williamsburg Bridge, not more than a few blocks away from Soft Tidings. The cause is still undetermined. I hope you can find comfort in my condolences as I did in yours. . . . Benjamin Ibo.' "

By the time Silvia had finished, a certain vindictive quality had crept into her voice.

"Today, *I'm* working for Soft Tidings," she told Heller.

Heller was unresponsive. It was almost comforting how little he felt, the complete lack of anything inside him. Silvia matched his silence. Heller let the air out, felt something rush into him with his next breath. A small, compact ball of something inside of him, fed by the very fact that he was alive. Whatever it was, it grew with every breath, even as he stood there, doing nothing, just standing in his room without a shirt and the afternoon sunlight spilling over his bare feet.

Heller walked over to the nearest wall and tore down one of his posters. It was a completely visceral action, the experience absolutely sentient. The sound of the paper ripping, the sight of a bare wall underneath, how it felt to crumple that image of a world-class cyclist into a meaning-less little ball.

Silvia's messenger facade wavered.

Heller was hardly aware of her watching him. In slow, trancelike motions he made his way around the room, be-gan to bring down the rest of the posters, repeating the process, with each one his thoughts growing more suscept-ible to what Silvia had just done.

The favor returned.

Heller strode over to his shelves, gaining momentum, knocked his bicycle models and figurines off their stands, some actually landing in the garbage. He walked to the edge of his bed, sat and took his copy of *The Aeneid*, began tearing out the pages.

Silvia finally spoke. "This is no way for you to honor a dead friend."

Heller's eyes shot up, back in the room for the first time.

He reached under his pillow and pulled out his copy of *Don Quixote.*

Opened it to the title page and ripped it out.

He glanced up from the book to check her reaction.

All he saw was a spark of confusion.

Heller looked back down at the book and saw Silvia's picture there, lying on the first page of text. He picked it up, stared at it for a long time, a memory that didn't belong to him anymore, never had in the first place.

Still looking down, Heller extended his arm, offering Silvia the picture.

She walked over and took it from him. She held the picture to her face, recognizing it.

Tears welled in Heller's eyes. "I didn't want to be the one to tell you," he said.

Heller began to cry.

Silvia stood by and watched him.

Heller dug his face into his hands and cried. He felt as though he might never stop. There seemed to be nothing to hold on to, and he cried until his face was more liquid than skin, eyes swollen to the point where they might as well be closed, jaw contracting with the stress, sustaining the pain of a friend he would never see again.

Heller cried, and each time he thought it would stop, it started over again, each sob a reminder of why it was there, and it kept on and on . . .

. . . and gradually, it subsided.

The tears stopped, the sobs became isolated hiccups, and a slow ache spread through his body, along with a new-found silence.

Silvia hadn't moved.

Heller closed the book and put it aside.

"It's going to be all right, maybe," Silvia told him. There was no way to tell if she meant it, if she cared, but she said it anyway. "Maybe it'll be all right, someday."

Heller sniffed, nose dripping. "You went to Soft Tidings looking for me?"

Silvia thought about it.

She held up the picture. "I went to Soft Tidings looking for this."

She dropped the photograph into her purse and walked out.

Heller heard the apartment door open and close.

He let out a shaky breath. The remains of his room surrounded him. He slowly stretched himself out on his back. Before he could ask himself how such a thing was possible, he was asleep again, only this time, there were nightmares.

chapter fifty-five

Two days later saw Salim cremated in an inexpensive ceremony.

Everyone involved in the search was seated among the cheap chairs of the crematorium, witness to the final rites. The morning washed in through a few windows.

The door to the oven opened, a gaping mouth.

Salim's coffin was pushed into the flames.

Heller stood at the front of the group, dressed in a mismatched suit, wearing a tie he had found in his grandfather's closet. He read from a book Velu had given him the previous day, a poem by Nazim Hikmet.

"*I*
Want to die before you.
Do you think the one who follows
Finds the one who went first?
I don't think so.
It would be best to have me burned
And put in a glass jar.
Make the jar
Clear glass,

So you can watch me inside . . .
You see my sacrifice: I give up being earth,
I give up being a flower,
Just to stay near you.
Then, when you die,
You can come into my jar
And we'll live there together
Until some dizzy bride
Tosses us out.
But by then we'll be so mixed together,
We'll fall side by side,
We'll dive into the earth together.
And maybe a wild flower will appear."

Heller closed the book and returned to his seat. Faced no applause, just the thoughts of the rest, and for what was left of the ceremony, focused on his own.

And it was a simple, transparent jar into which Salim's ashes were put.

The undertaker handed it to Heller.

Everyone got up to leave, a slow stream exiting. Each person gave Heller their condolences, handshakes, varying degrees of hugs on their way out. Heller responded accordingly, knew that the momentary somberness was all in passing, that it wouldn't be long before he remembered that the ashes in his arms were once a human being.

Heller's grandparents approached.

"The tie looks good on you, Heller," Eric said.

Heller understood. "I think I'll keep it."

Florence gave him a hug. "Do you want us to wait for you?"

"No, thank you."

"We'll be at home," Eric said. "Could you please call if you're not coming home soon?"

"I will."

They left, and Iggy wandered up.

He didn't say anything.

"Shouldn't you be at work?" Heller asked.

"Believe it or not, we haven't gotten a single call today."

"I don't believe it, actually. . . ."

Iggy shrugged, at a loss. "The world's resting up, I guess."

"Yeah . . ."

"Richard couldn't take off work, despite it all. He sends his regards."

"Tell him thanks."

Iggy hesitated, then: "What happened between the two of you?"

"Truthfully?" Heller searched around, found no other way to put it. "I really don't know."

"My father wanted to come, but . . . you know how he is."

"Tell him thanks anyway."

"I will." Iggy nodded, shook Heller's hand, and walked out, the last of the rest.

Heller sat down in a chair, tried to make sense of things.

It wasn't working, and the undertaker approached him cautiously. He had an odd walk to him, as though the upper half of his body had a limp and his legs were perfectly fine.

"Sir," he said, "we have another party coming in. . . ."

Heller nodded, stood . . .

Left.

chapter fifty-six

The sun was murder that day.

Scorching. A desert posed as an oasis, and Heller was loosening his tie before even stepping out into the blazing heat.

Silvia was standing outside. Next to her was an old bicycle, rust growing on its handlebars and spokes. Heller was far too involved with the morning's events to be surprised.

"What are you going to do with the ashes?" she asked.

"I was thinking . . . just thinking about sending them to Nizima so she can have them. . . ." Heller finished loosening his tie. "But I'm not entirely sure that she loved him as much as Salim might have hoped, you know?"

"I know there must be a post office somewhere in the neighborhood," Silvia offered. "You can think about it on the way there."

"You working for Soft Tidings today?" Heller asked, suspicious.

"No."

"Oh . . ." Heller tried to give an edge to his voice. "So

you're not going to, like, walk me to the post office, then tell me my parents are dead?"

"Do you really want to bring this sort of thing up now?"

Heller really didn't. "No."

Silvia motioned for them to start walking.

They did, and Silvia rolled the bike cautiously alongside her.

There was no post office in the neighborhood, it turned out, and the two of them walked all the way to Washington Square. The fountain was out of order, and what water remained was slowly evaporating. The complaints of tourists reached their ears from every corner of the park.

"I don't even know Nizima's address," Heller told Silvia. "Don't even know what a rural address in Turkey looks like."

"Do you know where you can get it?" Silvia asked.

"Where did you get the bike?"

"Found it."

"Really?" Heller was incredulous. "You just found it?"

"I was out for a walk," Silvia said. "Debating about whether or not I should go to the ceremony. Then I saw the bike lying there in the middle of the street, just waiting to get run over. Like it was committing suicide." She put her hand over her eyes, tried to shield herself from the white light. "So I thought I'd save it. Roll it over here."

"You missed the ceremony."

"I had to wheel the bike all the way across town."

"If you had known how to ride it, that wouldn't have been a problem."

"I thought you might like to have it. Use it while you get another one."

"I don't know if I'm getting another one."

"You don't even want to try this one out, see how it handles?"

Heller thought about it. There was an aggressive energy in the park that day, and it was hard not to notice. He shook his head, held up the jar of ashes, said, "I have to take care of these."

"What am I supposed to do with this?" Silvia lifted the front wheel of the bike off the ground.

"I don't know. Use it."

"You mean ride it?"

"Why not?"

"How am I supposed to learn how to ride this?"

"I don't know," Heller said, a slight impatience stalking him. "Ask for help. Ask someone to teach you."

"I can't do that," Silvia insisted.

"Hey." Heller stopped, stood in front of her. "He's not coming back. . . ."

Silvia looked at him, a deep sadness running down her body with the sweat.

"I don't know what I'm supposed to do," she said.

"I don't know what you're supposed to do, either."

"What *do* you know?"

"I know how to ride a bike—you start pedaling."

"I'm going to fall."

"More than once," Heller told her. "Start pedaling."

Silvia contemplated the bike. "You want to help me onto this?"

Holding on to her, Heller made sure Silvia was resting

comfortably on the seat before moving his hands to her hips, keeping the balance. Silvia placed her feet on the pedals. Heller began to walk, pushing her and the bike forward with his free arm. The chain came to life and made dry clicking sounds. Silvia began to pedal, uncertainly. They advanced, bit by bit. People walked by, some ran, others coasted by on Rollerblades or skateboards, all calling out to Heller, recognizing him as the bike boy. Recognizing him despite the fact that his feet were on solid ground.

"Keep pedaling," Heller encouraged.

He let go of the bike.

He watched Silvia wobble forward for a few yards. She jerked the handlebars suddenly and fell to the ground. Heller stood still. Silvia sat up. There was a scrape on her shin. She held her leg, tears in her eyes.

She looked at Heller.

"Get up," he said.

Silvia didn't move.

Heller went to her side, stood over her.

"Get up," he repeated. "Let's go. Get . . . up."

Silvia picked up the bike and got back on. She looked at Heller, looking for more encouragement. Heller thought about biting his lip. . . .

"Does this mean I'm your boyfriend again?" he asked.

"You were never my boyfriend."

"Am I your boyfriend now?"

"No . . . All this means is that you are my teacher."

Heller smiled, but a look on Silvia's face put a stop to it.

"I promise you," she asserted. "That's it."

"I don't entirely believe you."

"Well, we're going to have to learn . . ."

Heller realized there was something missing and nodded sadly. "Start pedaling," he told her.

Silvia was about to speak when Heller cut her off. "You can tell me some other time," he said. "Go."

Silvia pressed down with her left foot, wound glistening red all along her shin. It looked as though she was going to fall again. Pumping her right leg, then her left, she managed to straighten the bicycle out and kept riding.

"Go," Heller said, and watched her cycle away, rounding the dying fountain once, then heading east along a side path and disappearing among the trees. Heller watched her leave him, wondered how long before he could get any of it back.

He looked down at the ashes in his arms. . . .

"You know what, Salim?" he said, now only sure of how uncertain it all was. "You know what . . . ? I need a gin and tonic." He paused. "Just for today," he said, remembering Salim. "I think God will understand."

Heller nodded to himself, then held the ashes close and walked south.

The sun was directly overhead, and it was likely that the entire population of New York felt as though they could reach out and touch it. The heat wave engulfed everyone, and nearby a skirmish broke out between two people. Their words were lost to each other and the fight turned physical, punches exchanged, both of them falling into the grass before the police had a chance to break it up. A crowd formed around them, cheering or disapproving or simply curious as to what was going on in the park that day.

Heller kept walking, thinking about everything that

had already happened. He didn't smile because he knew it was all right.

It's getting interesting now, Heller thought.

Thermometers across the city agreed silently, and couples in the park sensed it as they smiled through their kisses, serene in the midst of the burning city.

Picture this:

Ariel Dorfman is in his study at six in the morning, fresh from a shower, searching for a book on the history of India. He opens it to a dog-eared page. Takes off his glasses, chews on one of the ends.

The door bursts open, and in walks his son, Joaquin. Hair a mess, tired eyes, and clothes smelling like his favorite billiard club. Computer disk in one hand, copybook stuffed with printed notes in the other. He walks straight to Ariel's computer, prints ten pages, tosses them in front of Ariel.

"I'm going to sleep," says Joaquin.

"You've done a great job on chapter one. Chapter three is too dark."

"Dark is how I write, old man," retaliates Joaquin.

"What do you think of the name Velu for the Indian book vendor?" asks Ariel. "Famous rebel in Kerala. What do you think?"

"I think there aren't enough women interested in guys like me," observes Joaquin.

"And I think chapter three is too dark," replies Ariel.

"And I think your nose is too big," Joaquin snaps. "And I'm going to sleep."

"And I'm going to do a little rewrite on this chapter," says Ariel, smiling.

"See you at midday," says Joaquin, with a genetically similar grin, and plods off to his own house across town.

Ariel sighs, picks up a pen, just starting his day.

Try to picture this several hours a day, every day of the week, for several months.

Try to guess which one got in the last word.

about the authors

Hailed as a "literary grandmaster" by *Time* magazine, Ariel
Dorfman has received numerous international prizes for his
novels, plays, poems, journalism, and essays. He won both
the Sir Laurence Olivier Award and the Time Out Award for
Best Play of the Year for *Death and the Maiden.*

Ariel was born in Argentina in 1942 but spent his child-
hood in New York. He then moved to Chile in 1954, from
where he was forced into exile by a military coup in 1973. He
now lives in Durham, North Carolina, and is a professor of
literature and Latin American studies at Duke University.

Joaquin Dorfman was born in Amsterdam in 1979 on
the coldest night of the year. He opened his first play at
the Edinburgh Festival at the age of nineteen. He has just
finished his second novel and is in the process of moving
from Brooklyn, New York, on to new adventures.

The Dorfmans have also written two screenplays together.